Off Limits

Sincere James

"I do it with Ink!"........

SINCERE JAMES

Published by "I do it with Ink!" (USA) Inc.

First printing, August 2016

ISBN 978-0-692-76530-2

Copyright © Sincere James, 2012

All Rights Reserved

www.authorsincerejames.com

Note from the Publisher

Every person has their breaking point, and I guess I can say mine started when I befriended Michelle.

Michelle was a beautiful woman inside and out, or so I was led to believe...

Life has a funny way of showing you things about people even when your heart wants to believe something else.

Sin J.

The first encounter

Sincere lay there in Tyler's bed while reliving the events from earlier that day, contemplating how she was going to begin to fix the mess that patiently awaited her at home. While lying there the door slowly began to creep open. Pretending to be asleep, she dared not to move. She soon felt hands carefully moving up her body.

She didn't budge as the hand continued to move up her thigh towards her lower belly. She still refused to move or acknowledge the presence. The person exploring her body was none other than her best friend's husband, Chance. Realizing he wasn't getting anywhere he turned around and left just as quietly as he came. Sincere lay there both confused and startled, not really sure what to do or how to respond. Michelle was in the next room, which is where Chance seemed to have retreated too.

Chance entered his bedroom, and Sincere listened while they talked to one another. Could her ears be deceiving her? It appeared as if Michelle knew all along that Chance had made advances towards Sincere, all under

4

her direction. Sincere continued to lie there, trying to figure out how to leave their house, but she had nowhere to go. Only a few hours earlier her pipes had burst in her house and Chance had come to turn all the water off, which was how she ended up over here in the first place.

Did they have this planned all along?

Is this why Chance kept calling her while she was out on a date with David?

All these questions were going through her head over and over again. Suddenly the door swung open again, only this time it wasn't Chance; it was Michelle. Michelle walked over to her and began to poke her violently and repeatedly in her side until she got a response or acknowledgment. She snatched the covers off Sincere.

"Stop faking! I know you aren't asleep. Get up and come watch a movie with us!"

Reluctantly, she got up from the bed wearing the oversized t-shirt Chance had given her to sleep in earlier.

Sincere walked into the next bedroom. She quickly surveyed the layout: a nice room, she had to say. The bedroom was equipped with a gorgeous king sized bed and moderately priced furniture, with a 72 inch flat screen TV to match.

They had been friends for several years, yet today was the first time Sincere had ever entered her bedroom. Sincere quickly zeroed in on the unoccupied chair in the far corner of the room and hurriedly sat in it. As she turned her head towards the television, she was not surprised to see a porno starring 'Lock on it Willie' pumping in two different women at the same time. Willie yelled at the smaller framed girl to "lock on it, bitch" as he twirled her around to face him, his ten inches of manhood now standing in midair.

Sincere shrieked at the thought of performing the same act with Lamont when he finally came home in a few weeks. Back to the obvious situation at hand, it was very clear what was going on: they wanted Sincere to be their extra for tonight. While attempting to seem cool about everything, she was scared out of her mind.

Michelle and Chance began to kiss and undress each other as if she wasn't even in the room. Sincere remained focused on the television until it happened.

Michelle asked her to get in the bed with them. Sincere laughed it off.

"Naw, I'm good right here, but thanks anyway!" Michelle flashed a devious smile.

"What's the matter, you chicken?"

Sincere felt like she was in a bad dream unable to wake up. Yet, determined to prove she was no chicken, she got in the bed with them. She hesitated initially, but once she climbed in the bed with them everything seemed to fast-forward rather quickly. She was beyond a ball of nerves; her hands trembled as she began to touch Michelle's face. She forced herself not to make eye contact of any sort. She had now made it past the initial touching of another woman. Feeling a little bit more at ease, she then began to softly kiss Michelle's lips while pulling her closer. As Sincere continued to kiss Michelle, she felt a familiar sense of wetness forming between her own legs. Odd, yet she still continued to kiss her. She gradually moved her hands down to the small of her back, Sincere gently laid Michelle down on the bed and began to admire her nude body in the moonlit room. Sincere was no longer afraid to look into her friend's eyes.

Michelle nestled back on the large bed and slowly spread her legs apart as she slowly kissed and sucked on Chance's manhood. Chance turned towards Sincere as he whispered, "Kiss her!" Sincere stalled for a moment as Michelle parted her lips to make it easier for her to see what she about to taste. Sincere calmly leaned in to gently kiss Michelle between her legs. Not bad, she thought to herself while inserting two of her fingers directly into Michelle's exposed wetness. Sincere, now leaping at the opportunity to try pleasing Michelle orally, closed her eyes and placed her face directly in front of Michelle's nectar.

Chance watched closely with one eye open until his head began to roll back in a circular motion from the wax job his johnson was receiving from Michelle. Michelle moved her hands from the resting position, and, now exposing her wetness, placed them on Sincere's head, calmly pushing it exactly where she wanted it. All while she continued to polish Chance's manhood, awaiting the next move of the newest player in their bedroom.

Sincere began nervously licking Michelle, searching for the right rhythm. She thought to herself that it was nothing like she had ever imagined. The texture of her lips was soft, wet and inviting. She always thought the juices of another woman would be anything but good in her mouth.

Damn, thought Sincere, *was I wrong?*

Michelle's insides grew wetter and wetter by the second as Sincere continued to please her.

Michelle began to softly moan and squirm with pleasure just as Sincere's own body began to flutter and thump wildly inside. Sincere at this moment was completely turned on and truly wanted more of Michelle! She continued to follow Michelle's rapid body movements and sweet responses. The cries became music to her ears; she loved the sounds that bellowed from her. Just as Michelle began to shake and scream to the top of her lungs in total euphoric ecstasy, Chance pushed her away and asked Michelle if she was okay.

"Yes, I am fine," she said, drunkenly, and quickly pulled Sincere back to finish sucking on her clit. The more Sincere sucked, the more she felt Michelle's clit growing, expanding and getting harder and harder in her mouth. She noticed, while engrossed in pleasing Michelle, her own nipples are fully erect and in need of some attention. She placed Michelle's hands on her melon-shaped breasts, her nipples awaiting Michelle's lips to take them in one at a time. Sincere abruptly took this opportunity for another kiss.

Chance gathered from the responses Sincere had gotten from Michelle that she must have done a pretty good job. He went from sexually stimulated to pissed off in no time.

Sincere, on the other hand, continued to please Michelle any way she saw fit and tried to ignore the evil glares from Chance.

Now feeling ignored and sick to his stomach, Chance took several steps away from the bed toward the door. He managed to utter Michelle's name without any anger in his voice. He stuttered when he spoke:

"Michelle, my stomach hurts!"

"Go get some water!" Michelle replied quickly.

Feeling a bit humiliated he slammed the door behind him as he headed towards the kitchen! With Chance now out of the room, Sincere continued to explore Michelle's body with her hands and mouth. She eventually went back to sucking and pulling on her clit.

Michelle was now violently grabbing at the sheets, her screams well above a whisper. Chance burst back through the door to witness the serious tongue lashing being delivered to his wife. His pride fell beyond retrieval from hearing all of her moans and cries of excitement face-to-face. How can a woman make another woman feel that way? What had he been doing wrong, he wondered, as he stood watching angrily from the doorway. He was no longer part of the sexual escapade.

Michelle and Sincere continue to go at it for what seemed like hours, touching and kissing on one another, totally oblivious to Chance's glares of disgust.

Besides determining she was good at pleasing a woman's body with her tongue, tonight was also the night Sincere discovered she liked breasts. Michelle was every bit of a well-stacked 38DD. The left one even had a cute little mole under her left nipple. Sincere loved the way their bodies glided under the moonlit curtains.

Chance stood over them from the side of the bed with his dick rock hard and ready to plow inside one of them. Michelle was not big on penetration so she pushed Sincere over toward him for entry.

Sincere hadn't been with a man in almost a year, and it was a surprise to her body, to say the least. He entered her now with so much force she screamed out in agony. She attempted to run away but wasn't successful. He continued to deliver pain with each stroke. She paced herself as she took in all of Chance.

Michelle caressed her face while licking and sucking each of her breasts, careful not to show one more attention than the other.

Sincere soon had tears streaming down her face. Michelle stopped licking Sincere's right breast to make sure she was okay. She knew it had been quite some time since Sincere had been with a man sexually. Apparently, right now was not time for twenty questions, so she opted to just comfort her, but she wasn't willing to trade places with her either. Tonight was really all about Michelle having her way.

Thinking back, Michelle would always ask her why she was single, and Sincere would always respond with something about Lamont, her deadbeat son's father.

Lamont was Jay's dad. Sincere's first great sexual experience came from Lamont. He was the only man that ever made her body do the things it did when he touched it. Sincere's inner walls began to pulsate just thinking about Lamont touching her again, providing some additional flows of wetness.

Although she had vowed to stay single until he came back around, even if for just a short while, Sincere knew she was denying herself the right to be happy with someone that she could potentially love. But hey, she was young and dumb.

Chance pulled out, then hurriedly entered her from behind again. She screamed, not so much from the entry, but from the thrust he placed with each stroke, as if making a mark within her fragile frame.

Sincere, a petite lady with a caramel complexion, stood a mere 5 feet 4 inches and barely weighed 110 pounds soaking wet.

Oh shit, it hurt and felt good all at the same time, she thought to herself. Why had she waited so long to get some again?

Oh yeah, she and Lamont had a falling out, and he was locked up yet again! Boy, was this making her miss

Lamont badly! Sincere laid there in disbelief. She was actually enjoying fucking her best friend's husband.

Michelle continued sitting right there, watching as everything between them played out. Deep down, Sincere knew there had to be some unwritten cardinal rule about this shit. Then again, Michelle was the one that pushed Sincere toward him in the first place.

Sincere could no longer take it from behind, and she franticly tried to move away from him. Though she was failing miserably, suddenly she had an idea.

She seductively turned her head towards him and said "Let me ride that dick now!" Sincere climbed on top of Chance and began to fiercely ride his dick with little hesitation. She was now in control of each stroke and thrust. Chance's body grew stiffer and stiffer with each stroke. Sincere knew that feeling from anywhere; he's about to blow and it wasn't going to be inside her. Chance motioned for Michelle to take over.

Michelle had been watching from the corner of the bed. Her eyes were watching Sincere's every move, every glide and stroke as if looking for an opportunity to correct her. Her eyes were fixated on Sincere, almost in a trance.

Michelle finally set her sights on Chance and said, "So you're about to cum, huh Daddy?" Chance shook his head yes, unable to speak. He knew it was only a second before he released his load.

Michelle pulled Sincere off of him and immediately placed him in her mouth. Chance let out a sigh of relief as some of his milk seeped from her lips.

Sincere watched in horror and amazement all at the same time. Michelle placed all of him in her mouth and seemed to be enjoying every minute of it. Chance began to moan and shake while steadily holding her head on his dick, continuing to explode in her mouth. She had never seen that done like that before! She watched attentively. Sincere had done it to Lamont plenty of times but never like this; she always stopped before the milk came.

Michelle began sucking harder and harder as he finished releasing. She swallowed just about every drop of him while trying to not let anything seep from her lips. Damn, it was as if she was trying to get more to come out. Sincere was officially stunned.

Afterwards, they all laid down in the king size bed. Unbeknownst to Sincere, Michelle placed her in the middle on purpose. Apparently, Chance would be ready for his next round again relatively quickly, and Sincere was to be the object of all the poking tonight.

Not that Sincere could say she minded because, hell, Lamont was locked up yet again, so it would be beneficial for her to get as much as she could while he was away. As Sincere laid there next to Michelle, she found herself touching various parts of Michelle's body. Michelle's breasts were amazing to her.

Chance reached over to see where Sincere had placed her hands and moved them several times throughout the night.

Sincere couldn't believe this nigga was jealous, yet he has just fucked his wife's best friend. Sincere laughed it off. *I guess niggas are territorial like that!* She settled her head on Michelle's breast at some point in time as they all drifted off to sleep.

Chance awoke a few hours later to get ready for work. He woke them both up to let them know he had set the camera up on the dresser to watch if they were going to go at it again without him. He warned them not to!

They lay there asleep until he came back a few hours later. Once Sincere was fully awake, she found herself unable to look at Michelle, let alone talk to Chance. Sincere was well past uncomfortable. She quickly dressed and went home to wait for Chance to come fix the pipes in the wall that had burst the previous day.

No place like home

Finally back at home, Sincere was cleaning up the last of the water on the floor when she heard a knock at the door. It was Chance.

Sincere opened her front door to find Chance on her porch looking down at the cracks in the concrete. Neither of them could or would make any type of eye contact with one another. Chance mumbled under his breath, "So how are you feeling about last night?" She acknowledged she was now a bit uncomfortable around him. Not only had they been intimate as a group, he had also entered her body in more ways than one, and, most importantly, she had slept with a woman, one of her best friends, no less.

Now thinking back over the events of the previous night, Sincere had pleased his wife, her best friend, orally, and she tasted him and her all in the same night. An unfamiliar sickness began to form in the pit of her stomach as she held back the vomit that attempted to make its way out against her wishes.

All of the above were *off limits*; they had now officially crossed the line of being friends.

"How do we go back, if it's even possible, to the way it was without it seeming awkward?" she asked Chance.

"We can't." he said.

They sat and talked about it and got out the feelings of discomfort within each other. Michelle, on the other hand, was a whole different story. Michelle was her usual chipper self as of this morning when Sincere had left.

"Dammit," Sincere said after being informed that the part Chance needed to fix her pipes wasn't in stock. Because her pipes still weren't fixed completely, they both knew this would lead to yet another visit from poor Chance.

Chance stepped outside to order the additional parts he needed; he paced back and forth in the middle of the driveway, clearly agitated. The additional supplies wouldn't be available for pick-up until the following morning. *God dammit,* she thought to herself. That means she would have to go back to their house again tonight or go to a hotel with her children. Well, at least this time

19

there shouldn't be any extra stuff jumping off since all of their children would be there.

After Chance pulled off, Sincere took that time to get some of her personal affairs in order. Over the next several hours, Sincere went on with her normal daily errands and activities with her children. Throughout the day she tried to find a way to avoid going back to Michelle's, if at all possible. No such luck. It was the day after Christmas and all the local hotels were booked solid past New Year's.

As Sincere pulled in their driveway, Jay unbuckled his seat belt first. Their children always played well together, so it was nothing for them to be excited about spending the night.

Chyna, Sincere's youngest, was reluctant to get out of the car at first until she saw that Christa, Michelle's daughter, was also home. Chyna and Christa were both eight years old, so that was another plus. Jay walked in the door, dropped his overnight bag, kicked off his shoes and dove onto the couch next to Christa.

For Sincere, walking in their house had lost that comfortable feeling it used to have upon her entering it. Sincere was stunned to find Michelle bouncing around as if nothing had happened the night before, let alone them being intimate.

Michelle was bouncing around, smiling and grinning from ear to ear. Her giddiness was very noticeable to Chance also; he mumbled under his breath, "This overly happy bitch right here!" Before anyone could comment, Chyna said, "I like this Ms. Michelle. Mommy, she's really happy today!"

Sincere just shook her head and smiled back. Her new behavior was apparent to the children as well. They asked for snacks like crazy, since she was in a giving mood all the children took full advantage.

Over dinner, Michelle talked nonstop about pointless shit, merely just to hear herself talk. Sincere sat mostly in silence as Chance made new sculptures out of his silverware. Emotions seemed to cloud every inch of his face, as if he was reliving the night his wife slept with a woman, play-by-play in his head. Sincere wasn't sure how to perceive it at first but opted to not allow it to bother her.

The night went by without any further incidents. Michelle must have had trouble sleeping; she was up fixing everyone a big breakfast at quarter past seven.

Her smile was now completely gone. Sincere initially thought she could have still been sleepy until she thought she noticed that Michelle had a serious knot on the side of her head, which she was trying to hide under her hair.

Not wanting to start anything or make something appear that wasn't, she brushed it off and packed up everyone's overnight bags and left right after breakfast.

Chance arrived on time as promised to repair the pipes. Sincere could tell he was bothered by something; he barely uttered three words to her the whole time. Not that she cared, but in a sense she did. Several days had now gone by, her pipes were fixed and everything seemed fine and even back to normal.

Sincere was getting ready to cook dinner when she got a call from Michelle. Her voice was low and she spoke almost in a code she wasn't familiar with. Straining to hear her, it sounded like on the other end of the line Michelle was telling her they couldn't be friends anymore because she's having some weird feelings about what they did. Sincere, enraged by what she heard, screamed through the phone, "Bitch, are you for real!"

Sincere paused. She was taken aback by what she said, and quickly apologized for calling her out of her name. But, what the hell, she was pissed off.

Who and what gave her the right to say this after she and Chance had made their peace with it?

Michelle was now feeling bad about what they had done almost a week after the fact. Not to mention she and Chance had settled their differences on being uncomfortable around each other only days before.

What the hell? Was she serious? Who was she to decide this shit now? All of those questions ran through Sincere's mind simultaneously. She tried to sound calm when she asked Michelle why it took so long for her to become uncomfortable or wierded out by the situation.

As usual, Michelle had no justifiable explanation outside of, "Because I do now!" Michelle was selfish like that at times, and in her mind her word was law. She wasn't going to change her mind unless she was the one to do it.

Sincere respected her decision, even though she didn't like it. Michelle was the person she talked to several times a day. She knew she would miss her even if just their conversations. Michelle was her confidante and true ride-or-die homie. Sincere shared many of her most personal things with her. Now it appeared to be dead and gone over one night of heated passion through *her* orchestrating. With each passing day, she hoped Michelle would reconsider. Days continued to pass with no word from Michelle.

This time Sincere guessed she must have been serious. Sincere grew to accept the decision, no matter how badly it hurt on the inside. Damn, almost a month had gone by since Michelle had ended their friendship. Sadly, this wouldn't be the first and possibly not the last.

Finally, out of the blue Michelle called in her usual cheerful voice. Sincere could almost see her smile through the phone. Unable to hide her feelings, Sincere grew excited and moist at the mere sound of her voice. They talked for hours just like old times.

Sincere had so many questions brewing inside her that she really wanted to ask, but she decided against it, at least on that call anyway. Why her? Why then? Why didn't she ask her first? Why end our friendship afterwards instead of talking about it first?

Sincere felt she was at least owed an explanation for the hell she had been through. If she ever had any doubts before, at this very moment she learned Michelle was really fucking selfish and stubborn.

Shit, she guessed it must be just an Aries thing!

Michelle gave Sincere no solid explanation for her actions. Michelle rattled on about her and Chance's role-playing with Sincere in the past. Sincere asked confusedly, "What the hell is role playing?" After Michelle explained what it was, she followed with more questions. "How do you role play without the person in the room?" Michelle explained to a dumbfounded Sincere what it was. Sincere only became even more confused than she was before Michelle explained it. Sincere asked in a shaken voice,

"How long had you been planning this?"

Michelle responded by saying, long enough to finally carry it out. Sincere paused and then asked,

"Why didn't you at least tell me what you were planning?" Sincere thought that since they were friends she should have at least been forewarned. An eerie silence took over the phone; a person would be able to hear crickets in the neighbor's grass several houses down. After the eternal silence, Sincere allowed her confusion to subside, since it was very apparent Michelle wasn't going to answer any more of her questions. They continued to talk about their children, then it happened. Michelle indicated she wanted them to do it again, only this time just the two of them, no Chance.

Sincere stumbled and choked on the phone, then smiled while trying to sound nonchalant. "Really, are you serious?" she asked, hoping to hear the right answer. Once the words, "Yes, I'm serious," rang through the line, Sincere exhaled a sigh of relief.

They began planning to do it again, setting a location and a date. Sincere liked the sound of being with Michelle again. One would say, judging by how wet her inner walls were becoming, her body did as well!

Falling for a woman

Sincere couldn't believe it, she was actually getting excited about seeing Michelle again. The mere thought of touching and tasting her again put her on an emotional high. This time would be different, she told herself, she would be better than the first time: no nervousness, no Chance overseeing what she was doing, to please his wife however she chose.

Sincere was overly excited and nervous all at the same time. Neither Michelle nor Sincere realized this encounter would be setting the tone for the years to come.

They planned to meet up in the next few days to do it again.

Sincere often wondered if she was gay now or just bisexual.

Michelle and Sincere met up at a secluded hotel for some alone time. They were careful not to arrive at the same time or use their cell phones just in case Chance was watching or following them.

Once in the room, they were both nervous and unsure of what to do. That feeling dwindled as fast as it came. They began to kiss each other with more passion than either of them had ever experienced with any man.

Why was this touch so welcoming? So wanted and desired?

Sincere craved more of her with each and every touch. They fell onto the bed, still kissing and fondling one another. They were tearing at each other's clothes hastily as if this moment would be the last time for either of them to feel this way. Michelle laid back on the bed towards the headboard and awaited her touch.

Sincere started at her lips, slowly kissing her, moving down to her breasts and becoming very familiar with them. They were light-colored melons with nipples larger than life. Michelle's body responded happily to each suck, tug and stroke of the breast. Sincere carefully examined her breast while slowly sucking the left nipple first. Feeling her nipples harden, Michelle slowly arched her back.

As her body began to beg for more, Sincere slowly began to kiss her stomach and moved gently down to her awaiting wetness. Sincere paused when she saw Michelle was already extremely wet from anticipation, and so was she. Sincere reluctantly parted her lips with her tongue and began to move it slowly around, following her body movements.

Michelle began to moan softly, and the sound grew increasingly louder. Sincere was aroused as she began to softly tug and pull at her clit. She screamed with delight and Sincere's invisible wings began to take form.

Sincere was pleasing one of her best friends, and she seemed to be pretty good at it. She again began to question in her mind if this made her gay or bisexual. She quickly pushed those thoughts out of her mind and continued to live in the moment.

The two remained entwined with each other for what seemed like hours, and she loved every second of it. Sincere had never felt this way about any one in her life.

Was this how good sex was supposed to be or feel like?

If it wasn't, it had to be pretty damn close! They lay there cuddling with one another when they realized they couldn't stay there forever, as they both had families they had to get back to before the day got away from them.

Sincere hated saying good-bye to Michelle, but she knew she had to. As they walked out of the room and said their good-byes, they were careful not to be seen by anyone. Michelle promised not to disappear on Sincere like the last time before they drove away in opposite directions. After that particular encounter it wasn't awkward at all; it seemed right. Everything just flowed from Sincere's body directly to Michelle's with no hesitation.

Sincere had become more and more comfortable with herself about her sexual encounters with Michelle.

She often wondered: how can something that felt that good be wrong? Sincere had been with men all her adult life and no one ever made her feel like this. The one man she was head-over-heels dumb for, Lamont, gave her multiple orgasms and a good stiff one at least three times a day. Even her greatest cry and flow of juices he delivered never could compare to the way she felt at that very moment.

That feeling made it clear as to why many said that same-sex relationships were *off limits*. Shit, it was as if whoever started it wanted to keep it for themselves.

Chance surfaced a few weeks later at Sincere's house unannounced and surely uninvited. Apparently, he and Michelle had an argument, and she disappeared. Angrily, Sincere looked at him stupidly and replied, "Michelle isn't here," then slammed the door in his face.

Michelle began to disappear more and more, and Chance's visits became much more frequent.

It was almost time for Lamont to get released. Sincere didn't know the exact time, she only knew that the day had finally come. Not allowing their drama to consume her day, Sincere deep cleaned her house from top to bottom, ran several errands and got a fresh bikini wax to prepare for Lamont's return. Sincere didn't care about the hour of his release. All that mattered to her was that he was finally on his way home to her.

Lamont called to be picked up right before midnight. As Sincere made the trip to the bus station to get Lamont, she hoped maybe he would stay out this time. Once in the car Lamont opted to drive so Sincere could give him head as he drove back to the house. Sincere complied and took him slowly in her mouth. Reminiscing on watching Michelle give Chance head, she had learned a few things. Lamont squirmed and swerved all over the highway. Lamont excitedly screamed, "Shit Sincere, what the hell you been doing, practicing for a niggas return or what? That shit has been perfected!"

Sincere just smiled and said,

"I just missed you, Daddy!"

As they pulled in the driveway, Sincere noticed her motion sensor lights that lined her driveway were all busted and the motion light on top of the garage was gone. *Shit, so much for making sure everything was perfect*, she thought to herself. She decided not to say anything to Lamont right then. She wanted him to show her some attention in every area, and that would have truly killed the mood.

Lamont nearly flung the door off the hinges when he entered the house. He dropped his bag in the foyer and turned to Sincere and asked, "Can I get a kiss or a hug?" Lamont pleaded as he reached to pull Sincere closer to him. Sincere leaped in his arms and whispered,

"Daddy come get this pussy!"

Within an instant they were tearing at each other's clothes, which seemed to fall off instantly. Sincere was ready for Daddy's dick to go anywhere he saw fit at this point!

Lamont had been away for some time, but she already knew he was not a man to go without pussy for too long. She knew he was fucking the female guard up in San Quentin named Nikki, but it didn't matter to her because he was back home with her now. Lamont was brazen enough to even introduce them on one of her visits to the jail.

She knew she had to get on her job and both fuck and suck him royally right at that moment. She had prepared her body for the best sex when thoughts of the broken lights flashed in her mind. Again, Sincere disregarded it as they walked towards the shower and thought nothing else of it.

Michelle was still missing when Chance made another visit to Sincere's house. After she and Lamont showered and finished round one, they laid in the bed ready to go at it for the second time. Sincere climbed on top of Lamont, and she was in mid-stream of riding Lamont's dick when they both were about to cum. He heard someone outside the bedroom window. Sincere, on the other hand, wanted desperately to at least finish what she had worked so hard to build and tried to pretend she didn't hear anything. Who in the hell could be outside my house, let alone my bedroom window, she thought to herself while Lamont was now clearly preoccupied with who was outside the house. Sincere knew the drill: she was expected to cum when he did, so this one she was saving just for him. He had a tendency to give her the best head after they managed to cum together. Out of all her previous male lovers, Lamont was the best. He was attentive to all of her body's needs and wants. He always made sure she was satisfied before he ever got off. He had the ability to make her cum at least three times before he got his first one.

Needless to say, they both missed the opportunity because Lamont tossed her off him and grabbed his 9mm from his holster and told her to get in the closet. Sincere refused to hide; that was her damn house. Sincere quickly walked behind him to the back door. Lamont opened the door and aimed right at Chance's head. They both stood stark naked in amazement. "Are you fucking serious?"

Chance had been spying on them the whole time. He saw the things she had done with Lamont! *All* the things she had done! Lamont continued to look at Chance, then turned to Sincere and asked who the fuck he was. Stuttering on her words, she finally uttered out,

"He's my friend Michelle's husband!"

"Michelle? Michelle, Michelle…oh, MICHELLE!" Lamont screamed. *"That one bitch you always talking about!"*

Lamont cocked his 9mm and demanded some reassurance from Chance to confirm that what she was saying was in fact true. Chance quickly explained that he couldn't find his wife, and he thought she and Sincere were fucking around again behind his back! Lamont looked at Sincere and said, "Damn man, you fucked a bitch and I wasn't invited? What the hell a nigga gotta do to be down? Sincere, you hear me girl?"

Sincere turned beet red from embarrassment and quickly walked out of the room to cover herself. Lamont and Chance exchanged a few more words before she heard the door close. Lamont walked back in the room with a sinister grin on his face, not uttering a single word, only continuing to grin.

Sincere sat down on the bed, not really sure what to say or do at this point. She never wanted him to know she had slept with a girl. The feeling now accompanied by being called a *dyke*, *lesbian* and *freak*, words she never wanted to be called if someone that knew about that side of her ever became her enemy.

Finally after what felt like forever passed, they went back to what they were doing before Chance so rudely interrupted them. In the bedroom now, Lamont's stroke was now different, like he was angry with her. Or maybe it was all in her mind. They both took their time to complete the first of many exhausting nutts this night. It seemed like rest or sleep wasn't going to be possibly tonight so Sincere took both of Lamont's balls in her mouth at the same time in an effort to have him get one good last one. He was finally getting stiff and this nutt was well worked up. He quickly entered her from behind and slapped both of her ass cheeks simultaneously as his load erupted.

When morning came, Sincere was awakened by her cell phone ringing. Once again, it was Michelle saying she was okay, back at home, and once again that they couldn't go on. Instantly Sincere became sick to her stomach and dropped the phone. She swung her feet to the floor and made a mad dash to the toilet, only she missed. Shit went everywhere. Luckily for her, she had eaten pretty light the night before. She tried to think back to the events that morning while she graciously gave Lamont the best oral pleasure she knew how. Did one of his headless kids seep down her throat and decided they weren't going to stay? Or worse, could she be pregnant again? Oh shit, if she was pregnant who would be the father?

She was certain that Michelle had vacuumed Chance's entire flow before they came out, but then again they do tend to seep out on entry. Sincere let it go and chalked it up to her words, the night before and the massive fucking she had just endured from Lamont earlier that morning.

Michelle tried to stay true to her word and failed at every attempt. It seemed she liked the attention Sincere was giving her whenever they were allowed to be together.

Over the next month or so they found themselves dipping off for little excursions whenever they could sneak away from their family life.

Michelle had to be pissed at Chance when she slipped and told Sincere he had been following her around and was tracking all of their text and phone conversations.

Basically, he was watching their each and every move.

During one of the excursions, they were at Sincere's homegirl Keisha's house for some daytime play when

Chance popped up as Michelle was leaving. He jumped out of his truck, reached through her window and hit her in her face right in front of Sincere. Sincere was beyond pissed but wasn't carrying anything on her protection-wise at the time to protect either of them.

Michelle pleaded for Sincere to not call the police and promised to call her as soon as she could get away from Chance. As they drove off, Sincere knew it was only a matter of time before she was going to end it yet again.

Right on cue, the call Sincere dreaded but knew was inevitable came. Michelle's 'can't be friends' call was right on time. Once again she would end everything, only this time it would be for several months instead of days or weeks.

Keisha stepped in to try to help Sincere move on with her life. Keisha often explained to her that she couldn't keep putting her life on hold for a married woman, especially one with an abusive husband. If he hit his own wife, just imagine what he would or could do to Sincere.

She was the enemy to him, and he was man trying to save his marriage and family.

Sincere tried to appear as strong as she could even though she was terrified for her safety. Sincere always thanked Keisha for her concern and for just being there for her as she put moves in place to get her life back in order without all the extra chaos.

Finally, Sincere decided it would be best if she moved from the house that was only a few blocks from them and attempt to live a somewhat normal life without Michelle or their constant drama. Sincere needed to make things easier on herself as well.

She was under the impression she was in love with Michelle. *Yeah right,* she thought. She had realized whenever she was interacting with Michelle, she refused to date anyone else because she was totally engrossed in her and only her. However, to prove to herself she wasn't in love with her, she began dating again and really enjoyed herself.

Lamont

Lamont sat in his room reliving the previous events with Sincere and the whole run-in with Chance. Man, a lot had changed since he was locked up this last time. Lamont continued to dwell on the threesome Sincere had taken part in without him. In his mind, Sincere was his property whether he was with her or not. "How dare she allow another man to touch her without clearing it up with me?" Lamont said, flipping over his dining room table, which shattered as it struck the floor. He was hell-bent on revenge even though he had no real interest in Sincere since he was slowly getting on his feet.

Lamont knew how to get back in Sincere's good graces: sex, and lots of it was all he had to do. Lamont made the call to Sincere as if everything was all well between them. Lamont decided to use his son Jay to seal the deal for him to come spend a few days at her house.

He showed up the following day as planned, only he had more than a few days' supply of clothes; he appeared to have all of his belongings in small white trash bags and that killer smile plastered on his face as he was greeted by Sincere, Chyna and his son. "Daddy's home!" he said as he looked directly at Sincere. She wasn't thrilled but she loved Lamont, or so she thought. She only loved one thing about him, and if it was about sex, she knew she could have found better without all the headaches afterwards.

Lamont dropped his clothes in Sincere's bedroom, then trotted off to play Xbox with Jay in the family room.

Sincere wasn't sure if she should be excited or upset; this clearly wasn't what she had agreed to over the phone.

Lamont enjoyed the time with the kids, he just wasn't father material, to say the least. Lamont was accustomed to living off women due to his stunningly good looks, killer smile and amazing skills in the bedroom.

Sincere decided to address it with Lamont after the kids were asleep for fear of it turning into a huge argument, and she wanted some of him that evening after all. She finished preparing dinner and for the first time in years they actually ate as a family. Sincere smiled to herself as she looked around the table and saw Jay interacting with Lamont. Jay seemed excited to have his dad right there as he shared his day and missions they completed on the Xbox.

Chyna smiled as she looked at Lamont. He always treated her as his little princess when he was around her, even though he wasn't her biological father. It made no difference in how he treated them when he decided to play "Daddy". Sincere began to grow anxious as her body began to ache, awaiting Lamont's touch.

She took her foot and glided it up Lamont's leg until she landed right where she wanted it, letting Lamont know exactly what she wanted from him. Dinner was then cut short as they both began to yawn simultaneously while they glanced at the clock. It was striking really close to 9 p.m., which Lamont knew was the kid's bedtime for as long as he could remember. Lamont said, "Well, it's bedtime guys, I will see you all in the morning!" Chyna and Jay both got up without incident and trotted off toward their rooms as Lamont followed behind then to tuck them both in their beds for the night.

Chyna always tried to keep him in her room the longest, as she was used to him being gone when she awoke the next morning.

Sincere cleaned the dinner dishes as Lamont played 'the good father' with the children. She knew it was usually only a matter of time before he disrespected her, her home, or he got in trouble and landed back in jail. So she just decided to live in the moment and hope for the best while expecting the worst.

Lamont surfaced from the back of the house, watching Sincere load the dishwasher with the last few dishes. He began to undress her with his eyes as he headed over toward her. She remained bent over with her ass up in the air. Lamont stroked himself as he pulled her dress up, revealing nothing else to bind him from entering her.

Lamont rubbed her clit, testing for wetness. Sincere jumped as he attempted to force all of him in her. Lamont took his two fingers and placed them in his mouth for wetness, then reinserted them into her for the desired feel he was going for. Lamont leaned Sincere over the kitchen counter as he continued to play with her increasingly wet nectar, his fingers remained inside her as he stood stroking his manhood while he prepared for his true grand entrance.

Now ready and dripping with wetness, Sincere began to beg for more. Lamont removed his fingers and forcibly inserted his manhood. As Sincere began to moan, he looked around for something to muffle her cries. Unable to find something close, he looked at her dress and snatched it off of her in one yank and quickly inserted it in her mouth.

While Sincere was naked and completely exposed, Lamont took full advantage as he continued to thrust all of him in and out of her. Her moans turned into outright screams as Lamont held her bent over the counter, unable to move or flee. Not wanting to wake the children, Lamont picked her up while still inside her and casually walked toward the bedroom. Once in the bedroom he removed the dress from her mouth as he laid her on the bed. Sincere knew what this meant: he wanted some oral attention. So, as directed she obliged and slid off the bed and got on her knees. Surprisingly, he didn't want her to please him orally; he wanted her on all fours for his personal favorite, doggy style.

Sincere hated this position, as she had no control whatsoever; however, she went along with it. Lamont continued in this position until he was personally satisfied, then wanted oral pleasure.

Lamont slowly pulled himself out of Sincere, then placed her on her knees. She opened her mouth and tried

44

not to gag--he was still controlling how she pleased him instead of allowing her to go as she normally would.

He was a pissed off man on a mission, and she wasn't in on it. Each time Sincere touched him, he had visions of Chance touching her and it continued to anger him. Lamont decided tonight would be about showing her what happens when his *property* steps out on him. Though the true lesson was yet to be shown.

Visions of Michelle pleasing Chance danced in her head. Given the neck roll she saw Chance experience, she decided to mimic it to the best of her ability to see if she'd get the same response. He felt the sucking was drastically different but he liked it; he knew she was thinking about something or someone else. Rather than get angry, he went along with it, as it was much better than she had ever done.

Just as he was about to blow, Sincere pushed Lamont back on the bed and climbed on top of him for the explosion to be inside her rather than wasted on the floor.

Lamont knew that was one of her rules; she would never swallow or have it sprayed on or anywhere near her face. That was where she and Michelle were completely different.

Sincere took that as beyond disrespectful; it was just fucking nasty, to say the least. As Lamont begin to erupt, he gripped her ass cheeks and squeezed tightly and exhaled loudly. Both of them were now exhausted and decided to call it a night.

She cleaned herself and then climbed in the bed to find Lamont texting someone with his back towards her. *Okay, so this nigga is still on this dumb shit,* she thought. No worries, she knew this was how they had been rolling for the past several years. Lamont was not and could never be a one-woman man. Sincere looked over to see who he was texting. Nikki, she knew that name from before but initially couldn't recall directly who it was.

Nikki, Nikki, oh Nikki, she thought to herself. Nikki was one of the guards from he was in San Quentin this last time.

When did they start talking again, or had they never stopped? Yep, the old Lamont was back full throttle; he was just using Sincere for a place to stay until another offer came along that would pay off a little better. Sincere decided to not ponder on it and went to sleep. In the morning she would tell him he had to leave after the kids went off to school.

Sincere awoke to the smell of something burning, which smelled of bacon or toast. She jumped out the bed to find Lamont in the kitchen attempting to cook the kids some breakfast and was burning everything. She peeked around the corner, snickering to herself as he tried to cook on her stove. Sincere stepped out to be seen and laughed as he continued to look confused while making his version of an omelet in the George Forman.

Jay was infuriated with Sincere for laughing; he knew these moments were few and far between, so he enjoyed the haphazard attempt at cooking. Lamont flashed that smile and Sincere decided not to ask him to leave just yet. She figured he would leave on his own, so why bother speeding it up. Jay loved his dad being there when he woke up. He knew his father wasn't the best father, but he was still his father. He continued to frown at Sincere after she entered the kitchen.

After the disaster at breakfast, Lamont helped get the kids off to school. Sincere dressed and got ready to head in to the office. Lamont agreed to stay while the ADT installer came to install the new security cameras in the media room Sincere was creating for the children.

After several hours of waiting, the installer finally knocked on the door. Lamont, steaming after being there all day, opened the door to find Chance in full gear to install the new equipment. Chance and Lamont stood there, staring at one another in anger, then shook it off as work and Lamont let him in.

Chance went straight to work as he chuckled every now and then. Lamont was intrigued to know why this nigga was laughing and if it was directed towards him. He straightened up and let Lamont know he was laughing at the situation, not him as a whole. Lamont looked at Chance and said, "Do tell my nigga?" Chance went on to say he was just thinking back to how they initially met at the old house.

Lamont, not finding it funny at all, stood with a scowl imprinted on his usually smiling face. Chance took notice and quickly went back to work. Lamont heard a knock at the door and went to let his *guest* in. Lamont returned with Nikki on his arm. Chance looked Nikki up and down in amazement and gave Lamont the head nod as if he was in agreement to what was about to go down.

Nikki smiled, held on to Lamont, and whispered,

"So how much time do we have before she comes back?"

Lamont, unmoved at the possibility of Sincere walking in on him, shrugged his shoulders as if to say *who cares*. Chance looked on in disbelief and worked to hurry up and get out of there before the shit really hit the fan. He was finishing up the last camera, then Michelle called him to get his twenty. Chance closed off the last line, announced he was finished and let himself out as he heard soft moans coming from the bedroom.

Once outside, he told Michelle where he was and what was taking place in an effort to make his wife mad enough to where she would never mess with Sincere again. She was mad all right, but not at Sincere. She was disgusted and angry at Chance for telling her such lies and abruptly got off the phone with him and called Sincere.

Sincere ignored the first three calls then the text came across that read:

Sin, get home! Nikki is in your house, fucking Lamont in YOUR HOUSE, IN YOUR BED! Sincere dropped her cell, frantically grabbing her stuff and raced home. She parked a few houses from hers to catch him in the act. She hoped for her sake this was a cruel joke Michelle was playing on her for ignoring her calls. She crept in her own house like a thief moving about trying to not be detected by the homeowner. She entered through the patio door with ease. Upon entering she heard the screams of a woman. Slowing creeping towards her bedroom, she noticed her bedroom door was open as if she was supposed to see everything that was going on.

Sincere's mouth hit the floor as she saw Nikki was buck naked in her bed with Lamont's head buried in between her legs, pleasing her orally.

"What the fuck!" Sincere screamed, going for her Glock 45 caliber in the closet. Hearing the boxes falling over in the closet, Lamont scrambled to get dressed, tossing Nikki her clothes in the process. Sincere retrieved her gun and fired a single round only inches away from Lamont's head.

"Get the fuck out of my house and don't you ever call me again!" she screamed.

Sincere turned to see Jay and Chyna had just came in the door from school. Jay stood in complete silence as he starred at Nikki and Lamont in the bedroom hurriedly getting dressed. Unable to move past, Sincere stood between the dresser and the door of escape.

Chyna ran to the phone in the kitchen where they had shared the morning memories with *Daddy*, only to have a real-life nightmare playing out in front of them. She reluctantly called 911 for fear of her mom going to jail. Before she could dial the last number, there was a rush of police entering the house all at once. Apparently the neighbors had called the police themselves at the sound of the gunshot.

Sincere was instructed to drop her weapon and she complied, filled with hurt and anger. The officers took each of them in separate rooms to get their versions of what had happened. Michelle continued to call and text Sincere to make sure she was ok. Sincere continued to ignore Michelle. Not sure what to say out of pure embarrassment to the questioning officers, she simply hung her head in shame.

Sincere made up her mind: this was the ultimate disrespect and she was totally done with Lamont, no matter how good he was in the bedroom.

Nikki was allowed to leave without any incident and was advised to not ever return to this residence, or any residence, occupied by Sincere or her children.

Lamont, on the other hand, wasn't so lucky. After running his name through their system, he appeared to have several outstanding warrants spanning six different counties. Seems after his latest release, he was to get his affairs in order and report to another county to face additional charges, and he appeared to be on the run.

Now in custody, Sincere wouldn't have to worry about him contacting her, at least for the time being; he had more legal trouble to face. Sincere was allowed to remain home with just some off-the-record advice to leave him alone for good. Advice she was determined to surely follow going forward.

Once the scene was cleared out, Sincere checked on her children. Jay was angry at both his father and his mother. Jay lashed out, then broke down and cried hysterically. Chyna was a ball of nerves at the sight of Sincere holding that gun to a man she loved and a strange woman. They had never seen Sincere so angry before, especially at Lamont. Sincere apologized uncontrollably to her children, then promised them they would never be exposed to something like that ever again. She kissed them and went to her bedroom and began removing the bedding from her bed, placing everything in a trash bag. After she placed everything in the garbage, she went to pull her car in the garage.

Jay was in the media room when she came back in the house. Sincere had completely forgotten about the installer coming. She began playing around with the cameras to see what was already recorded. Sincere came across playback mode, which allowed her go back to the completion of the installation, which was more than she expected. Chance's face flashed on the camera and she began to put two and two together. So that was how Michelle knew Lamont was there, because Chance had been in her home. *Dammit.* Sincere screamed. Now he knew where she lived yet again.

Brenda

In an attempt to get over Michelle, Sincere sparked a friendship with one of her coworkers, Brenda. Brenda was absolutely gorgeous; she was a mixture of Puerto Rican, black and Hawaiian, with long, flowing, black wavy hair, hazel eyes and a body any woman would kill for. Though visually exotic, she was also mysterious and classy. A much deserved and welcomed change from dealing with Michelle's many shenanigans.

They began spending a lot of time together. Brenda warmed up to the idea of allowing her new friend to meet her first love, her son, Mason. Sincere was crazy about him instantly; he was the coolest little kid ever. He didn't need to be entertained like most kids his age; he kind of just did his own thing and kept himself busy. Sincere didn't care too much for how Brenda acted when she was going through something. In the beginning she ignored the warning signs. To help make things easier for Brenda, she opted to take Mason off her hands. She soon realized why Brenda was single. She was a "certified" fucking psycho to say the least. At times, she matched Lynn Whitfield's *Thin Line Between Love and Hate* role to a T. She didn't want Sincere talking to anyone but her.

In the beginning Sincere agreed to keep the peace, but then it was apparent she had some serious insecurity issues. Sincere learned of the jealous side during a typical day in the office when Brenda saw her talking to another female coworker longer than she wanted her to. Sincere, sensing Brenda staring, decided to test her and spoke candidly to the female coworker and soon felt the need to sit on her desk with her breasts bulging out of her shirt.

One would have thought Brenda had super hearing as soon as Tyesha bent over, whispering in Sincere's ear, because Brenda jumped up quickly and walked over to Sincere's desk to make her move. Tyesha, felt the tension, rubbed Sincere's hand and said, "Call me later when you are free to talk or just come by my spot." Sincere nodded while grinning in agreement and prepared to deal with Brenda. Brenda merely growled, walked away and went back to her desk. The remainder of the workday went on as usual with no additional interruptions or distractions. As they all packed up to leave for the day, Sincere was halted in her tracks when she noticed someone slashed all four of her tires right on the company property. *Really? This was a straight bitch move,* she thought to herself. Sincere hadn't seen or heard from Michelle, so she didn't think it was Chance.

Brenda offered for Sincere to stay at her house while she got her tires repaired. Sincere reluctantly agreed. As they waited for the flatbed to come get her truck, Sincere took this opportunity to feel Brenda out. She had never stayed at her house overnight before, so naturally she was a bit nervous. Brenda started in on questioning Sincere as to who she thought may have done this and why, or who did she piss off? Looking off into space, Sincere mumbled, "This all seems suspect to me, but I don't have a clue as to who could have done this!"

The tow truck finally showed up two hours later. Tired, hungry and exhausted all in one, she was eager to shower and lay down fast. Once at her house, Brenda put on some mood music as Sincere disappeared for a much-needed shower. As she washed herself, Sincere could clearly hear "Kissing You" by Keith Washington playing in the next room. Stepping out of the shower, Sincere noticed a glass of wine waiting for her. Where did it come from? She never heard the door open up.

Hurriedly she dried off now that Lisa Fischer's *How Can I Ease the Pain* was beginning to play in the adjoining bedroom. Brenda stripped naked and positioned herself in the middle of the bed to be the first thing Sincere saw when she exited the restroom.

Sincere slowly opened the door; she saw Brenda on the bed with her eyes closed, naked and seductively touching herself. Brenda was totally engrossed within her own realm to notice she had entered the room. Sincere gradually walked over the bed and began to kiss her heels, working her way to her calves, easing up to her thighs. She smiled as she made a mental note of Brenda's freshly shaved inner lips, along with the wetness flowing from within her walls. She would be the good lover today and start from the top before working her way back to the middle.

Brenda openly took her in her arms as Sincere pulled Brenda's thighs up to her sides. Sincere positioned herself directly between Brenda's legs to maneuver a slow grind, rubbing their clits against one another while kissing her neckline and thin MAC-trimmed lips. She loved this Brenda, the totally submissive Brenda, the less talkative one, the *pillow princess,* if you will. In Sincere's mind, less talk was better and the bedroom was the one place where 'mum's the word', unless cries of passion were being spoken. Although they had played house many times before, this time was almost bittersweet.

Sincere was all but convinced that Brenda had something to do with her tires being slashed at the office. She was the only person mad at her, but oh well. Sincere opted to fulfill her sexual needs now, then address it tomorrow. Tonight was the perfect night; Mason was visiting his dad and so were Sincere's children, so they had plenty of alone time. Brenda had cooked dinner for them and planned on watching a Tyler Perry movie prior to Sincere taking her shower.

No longer into the grinding of the bodies, Sincere proceeded to lower herself to a more desired location. Softly toying with Brenda's nectar, Sincere heard the buzzing of her cell phone on the window ledge. It was Michelle; she had the house to herself and wanted to reach out to Sincere. After the first text and call went ignored, Michelle began to text Sincere like a fool in love. She hated being ignored more than being away from Sincere.

Sincere refused to stop what she was in the middle of, as her wings had not yet taken form. The buzzing

repeated over and over until it fell to the floor. Brenda
pretended not to be annoyed by it, but it was written all
over face. Her excitement was written all over her face.
Sincere stopped concentrating on Brenda and just wanted
her to cum so they could hurry up to allow her a moment to
slip to the restroom. She knew it had to be Michelle
blowing her up like that.

Michelle did still have her heart, and this was the
writing on the wall right here. Sincere tried to play it cool
and finish as if she wasn't annoyed with her but was failing
miserably. Brenda was a true freak and Sincere loved all
the attention she gave her orally. Michelle didn't have
head skills anywhere near like Brenda, but she loved her
anyway. Brenda went down and served Sincere's body
enough to cover her for a good bit. Sincere's legs were
shaking like crazy; Michelle could never do that to her.
Sincere had to place a pillow in between her legs to stop
them from moving the bed so Brenda could drift off to
sleep.

Once Brenda drifted off to sleep, Sincere slipped
out of the bedroom and returned a few of the messages to
Michelle's cell and was surprised when she responded right
back. Michelle was trying to come and see her, but Sincere

knew she couldn't because she was over at Brenda's. Sincere could hear from her tone she was mad as hell. Michelle said, "I'm sorry for doing this to you and expecting you to stop your life for me!"

Sincere truly felt for her, wishing she could just hold her and tell her it was going to be okay. Brenda began tossing and turning in the bed. Not wanting to be caught on the phone, Sincere told Michelle she would get with her tomorrow morning when she was freer to talk.

When they awoke the following morning, Sincere quickly dubbed Brenda 'psycho-Annie' when she observed Brenda had an attitude once both her eyes opened up and her feet hit the floor. Sincere attempted to steer clear of her so they wouldn't be late for work. Damn, after last night who could wake up in a bad mood? Hell, maybe this chick is just not a morning person. One of the drawbacks of working with someone you fuck. If she decided to call in, that meant she was stuck too.

Luckily for Sincere, she didn't call in. Riding in the car with Brenda, Sincere thought to herself she would have had more luck hitchhiking with ex-cons today.

While Brenda made the drive into the office, she steadily increased her speed repeatedly; once they hit an excess of 90 in a 55 miles per hour zone. Sincere repeatedly asked her what was wrong. Brenda began to cry hysterically.

"I read your text messages from Michelle when you went to sleep. You told me you were through fucking around with her. Yet you said you missed and loved her in the text message you sent to her last night after you fucked ME!"

Sincere felt lower than whale shit at the bottom of the ocean for playing with her emotions like that, but, hell, what's done is done. She gripped the door handle in complete terror. Kissing the pavement, she thanked God that they had made it safely.

At the office, Brenda's ass did a complete Dr. Jekyll and Mr. Hyde turnaround. She was back to being nice and friendly. Beyond a whack job, she was a private person and refused to allow the office folks in her personal business. They generally took all of their breaks and lunches together, but after that horrific car ride to the office Sincere decided to eat alone. Just like that, Brenda flipped out again. *Damn, here we go again!* She calmly asked

Sincere to ride with her to the lake to walk around the lake. Sincere hesitated but then agreed. They arrived at the lake where Sincere soon found herself fighting for her life. Brenda had strong-armed her and attempted to throw her in the lake. She managed to break free and ran back toward the office in a desperate attempt to get away from her.

Brenda jumped in her car in a hot pursuit but must have thought twice about hitting her with her car because she swerved around her and kept going. Once back in the office, Sincere hastily got back to her seat to and tried to find another ride home. Sincere called the lot where her Tahoe was being repaired. *Dammit.* As her luck would have it, the damn truck still wasn't ready and wouldn't be until sometime the following day. Not only did someone slash all the tires, but they also poured Diet Coke and sand in the gas tank. Pissed off to the highest level now, Sincere was totally convinced it had to be Brenda that had done it. She slept at her house last night, and there was no way in hell she was going to ride back anywhere with Brenda. Scrolling through her cell, she decided to call her ex-husband Kevin to pick her up after work.

Kevin agreed to get her from work and also to take her to Brenda's after work to get the stuff she had left at her house. Kevin was a typical nigga; he arrived a few minutes late, but hey, beggars can't be choosers. Kevin turned to Sincere and said, "So tell me, what the hell happened?"

Sincere repeated the events from that morning leading to the lake when he burst out laughing hysterically. "Damn, what the hell did you do to that bitch? I told you that bitch was a no-no, but no, you said you got this. Well Brenda showed your ass, didn't she." Kevin continued, still laughing, "Shit girl, if I had known you would go get a bitch, I would have fought for you in the divorce. Hell, we could have made the shit work for real!"

Sincere wiped her forehead and closed her eyes. From that moment on she made a silent vow to leave females alone for good. Between Michelle, Chance and Brenda she surely had her fill of drama and everyone in it for a good long while. Keeping her promise on track, Sincere stayed to herself for a few months. When Michelle surfaced again it was Mother's Day, and she called like Sincere knew she would. Michelle started the call very happy-go-lucky, pretending she only called to say Happy Mother's Day and to see how things were going in Sincere's world.

Sincere couldn't front; she was elated to hear her voice. Deep down she always knew Michelle would call again. It was a true pattern between them. Sincere had even kept the ringtone the same, just so she would know to answer no matter who or what she was doing.

Michelle was always number one to her. The old Sincere was notorious for changing her number, and this time she hadn't changed it for quite some time. She had to keep the lines of communication open for Michelle. Michelle filled Sincere in on what had been going on in her world, and Sincere obliged and did the same.

This time she couldn't have called at a better time, since Sincere had recently quit the job where crazy Brenda worked. Michelle had just informed Sincere she was the hiring manger for a prestigious firm where they happened to have an immediate opening.

They continued with idle chit-chat for a few more minutes. Glancing at the time, Michelle ended the call but promised to touch base the following business day about the position she had. Sincere smiled, wanting to end the call on a positive note, held back saying *I love you.*

That evening seemed to drag on forever and ever, but finally Sincere was able to doze off. The following morning she jumped up before the roosters had time to crow. She dressed hurriedly to get her children off to their destinations just so she could get more time with Michelle if she called back. Traffic seemed extremely light as Sincere pulled up at her children's school. Aw shit, all that rushing around for nothing; today is Saturday.

She knew she surely wasn't going to hear anything from Michelle today. No call on Saturday or Sunday! She had to admit she was disappointed, but hey, she did say business day, right? Not tomorrow. Looks like Chance still kept her on lock down on the weekends because her cell was off from 5 p.m. Friday until 7 a.m. Monday morning.

Business or pleasure

Monday rolled around and, as promised, Michelle called. Michelle had informed Sincere that she had found her a position. She told her how to dress, but she basically only had to show up for a gig paying $20.00 per hour, which was just opening the door for people while sitting at the front desk, smiling. Sincere thought, hell yeah, super easy money and it is not too far from where I now live.

Within a week, once again they were back creeping around again, only this time Sincere got paid to fuck her. Michelle was her boss, so that afforded her extra-long lunch breaks, late arrivals and early dismissals. She absolutely loved it. They would meet up several times a month for lunch break rendezvous. Michelle oftentimes would pick her up from the site she had placed her at.

Sincere would tell her the day before what to wear and she would do it. Michelle had this rose-colored skirt she would wear; Sincere absolutely loved it.

Michelle, like most women, required a lot of direction and loved compliments. She didn't mind being led when she wanted to feel powerless. They would do it anywhere they could! Whether it was in the back of her truck or in her office after 5 p.m. when everyone was gone for the day, they made it work within the time they had available. The thrill of getting caught made it all the better, even though they might never be caught. The sex in the office was always amazing; the things they did on the conference room table would make a porn star blush from envy.

Now that they were back on speaking terms, Sincere's personal life began to fall apart yet again; all the good shit took a hit! She stopped talking to everyone she had met again for her. Seeing that she was falling back into the same foolery, her closest friends even backed away from her when she refused to listen to reason.

Michelle began talking about leaving Chance but, as always, said the timing was wrong. Sincere began to see why women that cheat with married men stayed around, even if just for the possibility that the cheater might actually leave. Michelle had both Sincere and Chance wrapped around her finger. Whenever Michelle wanted to see her outside of their daily episodes, a threesome with

Chance was sure to be involved. Sincere didn't really mind because in a sense she got the best of both worlds. Chance and Sincere had finally gotten to where they would communicate about the three of them doing it without including Michelle, or so he thought. Sincere told Michelle everything and wanted to believe she told her everything as well.

Call her greedy, but Sincere often let Chance think it was his idea when she had already been with Michelle earlier that day. On one occasion Sincere showed up in just a teddy under her coat as Chance had asked. As he led her down the stairs leading to their basement, she was amazed to find Michelle dancing on top of the pool table with her eyes closed, completely nude. Michelle sensed someone staring at her; as she opened her eyes she was startled to see it was Sincere standing beside Chance. Chance grinned as he went back to secure the door. Michelle climbed off the pool table, and the pair held an intense conversation with just their eyes. Sincere knew that even if she had no real interest in Chance, if she wanted to see Michelle whenever and however she could, she had better play along and screw him as needed. They each took turns screwing and sucking him to keep the suspicion down.

The following morning he actually fixed both of the ladies breakfast in bed. They both showered and ate the food he had prepared for them, and then Sincere left for the day. Relieved to not get the phone call that typically came from Michelle after their group encounters, Sincere felt she could relax. Several days had passed when she received a call from Michelle; to her amazement, she invited her to lunch instead of talking over the phone.

Michelle decided today be the day she would open up to her friend about what really went on behind her closed doors. "My life is nothing to envy, Sincere," Michelle began, as she added even more intimate, private details about her childhood, ending with the first night of many nights her seemingly perfect husband began beating her. She rambled on and on about how he never paid attention to her, how he continued to run the streets instead of being home with her and the children, and having countless women leave bags of diapers on their door step.

Sincere felt tears forming in her eyes as Michelle continued to vent. She knew she had always tried to show her how much she meant to her and never hit her like he did. She surely never cussed at her, made her cry and would never ever cheat on her if they were ever allowed to be together. In Michelle's eyes, Sincere was everything he wasn't and could never be. Sincere made her feel special all the time. Sincere listened to her, noticed new haircuts, new makeup or clothes, all the simple things men took for granted. After all, in the end everyone wanted to feel special, get that one-on-one attention and most importantly to be noticed, right?

After lunch they each returned to their vehicles, heading in opposite directions. Sincere smiled as she approached the stoplight, fumbling in her purse to retrieve her cell phone that was now vibrating uncontrollably. She answered without bothering to glance at the caller ID; the muffled cries on the other end of the line quickly interrupted the pleasant thoughts of her lunch recap.

Son of a bitch, she strikes again!

The sobbing voice on the other end of the line was Michelle ending it all over again. They parted ways once again for almost a year for no apparent reason outside of her feeling bad; Sincere felt like an ass for falling for it again. Sincere took this time to really begin trying to determine if she attracted to all women or only Michelle.

So let the games begin.

Enter Shawnie ...

Sincere pulled into a local gas station to fill up her truck when a light-skinned babe with shoulder length hair walked past her, smiling. Sincere did a look around to see if maybe there was someone behind her, but there was no one there. Sincere continued to pump her gas with confusion written all over face. The mystery lady exited from the store and, determined to catch Sincere's attention, stood directly in her face with her hand extended as she introduced herself.

"My name is Shawntel but my friends call me Shawnie!" Sincere extended her hand as she replied,

"My name is Sincere and you can call me just that!" Shawnie laughed, then replied, "Cute, real cute!" Sincere found herself staring at her. Shawnie was absolutely gorgeous from head to toe. Sincere was by no means a stud; she typically dressed for comfort and today was no exception. She was dressed in a pair of short-shorts and a halter top with flip flops. Sincere had no problem complimenting another woman when it was warranted.

Shawnie, on the other hand, wore a formfitting maxi dress with a matching sunhat and a pair of heels. Sincere engaged in some small talk to get her to exchange numbers.

Before Sincere was off the lot, her cell phone was ringing. It was Shawnie already. *Damn*, Sincere thought, smiling to herself, *this one will be easy to get.* In the beginning, their conversations were brief and basic girly stuff, slowly progressing to more detailed stuff as Shawnie's interest sparked, and the questions began to roll one after another.

During one of their late night conversations, Shawnie asked Sincere to show her what they actually do in those relationships. Sincere smiled but was opposed in the beginning since Shawnie was what she often referred to as a "newbie," and that's stalker material. Shawnie laughed it off and said she wouldn't do anything any differently than she was already doing!

They planned to meet up over the weekend and play things by ear. Sincere continued with countless conversations throughout the week to get a feel for

Shawnie as a whole. As the weekend approached, Sincere was going to be alone and wanted some company, so she invited Shawnie and her daughters over for the night.

Sincere showed the girls around as Shawnie quickly made herself comfortable in the family room on the leather sectional. They watched movies with the kids until they all drifted off to sleep. Sincere decided to see if anything they had discussed was true. She knew Shawnie was curious, so why not test the waters and fill her needs at the same time?

Shawnie asked if it was okay for her to take a shower and get ready to lay down for the evening. Sincere took Shawnie up to her bedroom where Shawnie settled herself smack dab in the middle of her queen-sized bed after she got out the shower. Sincere took her shower in the hall restroom to allow Shawnie some privacy for now.

Once she finished down the hall, she peeked around the corner to see what she was doing and became aroused. Shawnie was slowly sucking on her two left fingers and parting her lips with her right hand fingers. She slowly placed them inside her and began to moan. Sincere quietly got in the bed, trying not to disturb her. Shawnie turned toward her, asking to be shown again.

Sincere played dumb and replied, "Show you what?" Now grinning like the cat about to smash the canary when no one is watching, Shawnie stopped stroking her fingers and said, "You know, what you did with the other women!"

Sincere thought there were pros and cons about newbies. She liked newbies for one reason only: the challenge! On the other hand, a newbie can also be a serious headache, because they can get sprung relatively fast off one or two good rolls around with a more experienced person. A newbie can also be dangerous if not handled the right way; it's a fast way to earn a stalker. Sincere proceeded to show her what she does, granting her request. She opted to skip the foreplay since she merely wanted to get it so she could be gone early in the a.m..

Sincere slowly entered Shawnie's overly wet lips with her warm tongue and went straight for the kill. No need in taking a lot of time to accomplish the desired response since she didn't love or really even like her, so no need in being patient with her. This encounter was clearly nothing more than a fuck followed by a *fuck you* later.

Shawnie began to moan louder and louder as she reached each level of ecstasy. Sincere's arrogance was becoming more apparent as she spared Shawnie no mercy. She had cum back to back several times when she started to cry and begged for Sincere to stop. Just like that, it was over and Sincere was ready for her to go after she cleaned her up.

The next morning, Sincere awakened to Shawnie serving her breakfast in bed. Again, her arrogance was not well hidden as she took the food in silence. Sincere found herself making comments to Shawnie that would have pissed her off had a nigga said the same shit after having sex with her the night before. If Shawnie was pissed off, she never showed it. The kids were now outside playing on the back deck when Sincere got a call on her cell. It was Stephanie!

Oh yes, little Stephanie was a young newbie and Sincere really wanted to go at it with her. Sincere was brazen enough to talk to her right in front of Shawnie as if she wasn't even there. Stephanie asked Sincere, "What's on your agenda for the evening?"

"Oh not too much of nothing, just gotta ditch this one that's already here!"

Stephanie laughed it off.

"Ok, holler back at me when she's gone and I'll be your agenda for the evening!"

"Right on," Sincere said as she ended the call, promising to call her within a few hours for her address to pick her up. Now even more agitated with Shawnie's very presence, Sincere scrambled to ditch Shawnie and the girls.

After everyone ate and Shawnie cleaned the dishes, they all got dressed for Sincere to take them back home. The drive back to Shawnie's was quiet the entire way between them. Sincere only spoke when it was necessary with very limited responses, surely no open-ended questions allowed. Sincere pulled up at her house, and Shawnie sent the girls in to the house to get settled in. She then turned towards Sincere and said, "Have fun on your lil date this evening and be careful. I would hate for your truck to have another mishap from you being a whore when it's not necessary!"

Sincere stopped fiddling around with her phone and gave Shawnie her full undivided attention. She was now listening to every word that came out of her mouth, remembering that she had told her about the tire slashing incident at the office. Shawnie also reminded her that windows cost more on a truck, with a devilish grin.

"Damn, you would really bust my windows, that's eight windows!"

"No sweetie," interrupted Shawnie, "There are nine so you better be real careful as to who you pick up from gas stations from now on!"

Now this bitch had Sincere speechless. Sincere sat there contemplating what to say and just replied, "Aight!"

Shawnie slowly got out the truck and walked back to her door quietly without looking back. Suddenly, she stopped dead in her tracks and came back and asked for some pocket money. Sincere quickly threw her a $50 bill for her troubles and drove off to get ready for her date with Stephanie.

Stephanie

While driving back home to get cleaned up for her rendezvous with Stephanie, Sincere thought about Michelle, Brenda, Chance and now Shawnie. Stephanie was ready to roll as soon as Sincere pulled up to her house. They cruised around for a little while, then Stephanie said,

"Show me your house!"

"Ok, cool," Sincere replied, grinning from ear to ear. Finally, she thought to herself to put an end to her wondering when she was going to get this one. A lot of people think *if* or *when,* but for Sincere it was just *when.*

She had proven herself to be a magnet. Women were coming on to her and she didn't have to do anything extra. After driving around the Bay Area for what seemed like an eternity, they were finally headed to her spot. As they pulled into her driveway, Sincere watched Stephanie from the corner of her eye. You can never be too careful, she always told herself, this one just might be the crazy one. The security gate opened slower than ever, but then again she had no need to rush; this one was going to be there until she took her back home.

Once inside the house, Sincere showed her around, leaving the bedroom for last. Stephanie questioned a few pieces of artwork she had on the wall. Though, it was just to make small talk on the surface. She appeared nervous and finally asked for a drink. Sincere smiled at her and said, "Well babe, there is juice or soda, no alcohol."

Stephanie paused, then asked for some water, obviously not one of the choices. No problem, that's what the faucet is for. After drinking a few sips of water she asked,

"So where is your room?"

Sincere playfully smiled and said,

"It's next, no rush, we have all night!"

Stephanie chugged back the rest of her water.

"Okay, let's go," she said.

"Alrighty, then let's go if you insist," Sincere replied. Stephanie followed Sincere's lead down the foyer and up the stairs. She stumbled and almost fell into a mirror on the wall. Once she gathered herself, she asked,

"How come you have so many mirrors going up towards your room?" Sincere shrugged her shoulders as if to say, hell I don't know, let's just get out of the hallway!

Sincere stood in the doorway while Stephanie looked around the bedroom and asked fifty million damn questions. Her eyes were fixated on the camera in the corner by the closet.

"So you make movies in here huh?" she asked.

"Yeah, well I've made in few in my day. Why? Don't tell me you're camera shy!" Sincere replied.

Stephanie must have felt Sincere was getting annoyed with all the questions, so she settled herself right in the center of the bed. As Sincere walked over toward her, Stephanie asked, "So what now?"

Sincere handed her the remote to the television along with the remote to the surround sound.

"It's up to you," she said with a sinister grin. Stephanie handed back the remote to the television, with an equally devilish grin as if to say *I don't need this!* After finding a station on Pandora, she began to lie back on the bed. Sincere moved toward her, then began to slowly undress her. She seemed impatient, almost a little rude even. Once she was finally completely undressed, Sincere slid away from her to turn on the camera. Stephanie quickly refused, not wanting to be another chick on film; surprisingly, Sincere complied. She climbed back in the bed and began to kiss her neck, moving down to her breasts, which were not too big and not too small, but just right for whatever one desired to do with them at that moment. Stephanie moaned softly. As usual Sincere's wings began to take form.

Stephanie opened her legs slowly for Sincere to make an entry with her tongue. As Sincere pulled on her clit, Stephanie began to moan louder and louder, just like the others. Sincere continued to suck, tug and pull on her lips as Stephanie's lips became dripping wet. Sincere moved her tongue up and down the walls of her nicely shaved nectar as Stephanie screamed with excitement. Her clit took form and Sincere zeroed in on it.

Stephanie began moving and shaking tremendously, and suddenly she began to squirt like a faucet. Sincere backed away from her in amazement, staring at her to what would happen next. Stephanie forced her face back into her wetness for more. Sincere continued until she begged her to stop. Stephanie wanted to try pleasing Sincere as if she was trying to work off her bucket list, carefully checking off each item line by line. Sincere laid back for Stephanie to try out her skills on her. She wanted to see if she could make her cum. Sincere had to admit that for her first time Stephanie did pretty good, and she swallowed, good traits to have. Stephanie now lay there motionless, which was beginning to irritate Sincere.

Dammit, how can I get rid of her? she thought to herself. Sincere retreated to the restroom and ran the shower. For sure this would be a way to wake her ass up and get her the hell out of here. When the shower was hot and steamy, Sincere jumped in and began to wash this one off of her. Stephanie got up out the bed to get cleaned up. Sincere was still rinsing off when the door slowly opened.

Stephanie was awake, and she was screaming on the inside. Sincere climbed out so she could have more space to herself. Stephanie showered for less than two minutes, like she was in prison. They both got dressed in complete silence. The entire trip to her house was also in complete silence. Sincere, blasting her music, didn't really invite much conversation. She pulled up in front of Stephanie's house, turning her music down to just above a whisper. Stephanie looked back at her.

"Sincere, you are going to call me again, aren't you?"

Sincere paused as if to choose her words carefully.

"Of course I am!"

As she pulled away from Stephanie's house, she pulled out her cell and began to scroll through her contacts until she found Stephanie's number, then selected *delete*. She laughed silently to herself as she made her way back home.

Michelle's return & departure

Michelle, being the one person Sincere would always drop any and everything for, decided to surface yet again. Chance jumped on her the night before, so she packed up her stuff and left. Michelle knew she was always welcome at Sincere's house, so she made that drive to the Bay Area in record time. Sincere invited her in and waited for Michelle to unroll the line of questions as to who Sincere had been with and who has been to the house and, most importantly, in her bed. Michelle was badly bruised and Sincere was pissed as hell at Chance for beating her flower.

Michelle desperately wanted Sincere to make love to her, yet Sincere was truly unable to. Sincere knew she had been with several different woman within the past 48 hours. Sincere decided to just hold her instead and explain to her the timing was wrong due to her current emotional state. Michelle agreed and didn't push the issue.

Sincere's heart bled for Michelle knowing she had been hurt and couldn't really seem to bring her true comfort. After talking a bit more they both decided to call it a night and drifted off to sleep. Sincere was jolted from her sleep the next morning to the sound of glass breaking in the foyer. It was Chance; he found Michelle and had come to take her back to their house with their kids.

He went on and on about how Tyler, their oldest son, missed his mother. Sincere tried to look at it from the kid's point of view and even from a family standpoint, but shit, she was just about to give in to Michelle's advances that morning and now this cock-blocking-ass nigga done showed up so she can't.

Michelle agreed to go back home with Chance and the kids and apologized for bringing drama to Sincere's home for the umpteenth time. Sincere had already begun to prepare herself mentally, as she knew the next communication from Michelle would be her telling her they couldn't be friends anymore again and, as always, she was sorry. Like clockwork, it happened; instead of a phone call this time, she got a vague text message, followed up with an email telling her it's off and she meant it this time.

Sincere read the text message and the email over and over again as if she just received it.

Sincere,

I really care about you and our friendship. I need to concentrate on my family and my marriage. I hate to keep disrupting your life like this. I promise, this is the last time I will bring drama to you or your home ever again!

143

Michelle

Sincere became angry and vowed to never speak to her ever again. Over the next several months Sincere became very engrossed in her work and with her own family. Her children were growing up fast and she refused to allow the remainder of her youthful days to be ruined by a basket case of a not so true friend. Sincere was forced to move to various parts around town as it seemed every time Michelle disappeared Chance assumed she was with her. Chance had friends everywhere to track her movements. He had friends at the license branch, the cell phone company and the banks where she did her business. Sincere soon felt like she couldn't do anything with him lurking around. Whenever they had problems and Michelle fled, Sincere would end up with the unwanted visitor outside her house, watching and waiting for the right opportunity to make his presence known. She would often arrive home from work or after hanging out with her children to find notes on her door from him. On one occasion there was a note with a rose left directly in the middle of her bed telling her he was sorry, he had missed her. This was more than enough, and she finally called the police to make a stalking report. She truly was living in Hell on earth and had no way out.

Nearly a year had passed since Sincere had heard from Michelle, but with her birthday approaching she knew it was only a matter of time before she resurfaced. She always had a way of contacting Sincere on holidays and birthdays. Sincere missed her tremendously; each time she heard the ringtone specifically for Michelle, her heart dropped. Sincere felt her ringtone was perfect for her feelings toward Michelle, Beyoncé's *Dangerously in Love.* Sincere's heart would literally skip a beat whenever she heard that song play.

Michelle called as planned on Sincere's birthday and wanted to meet and touch base. Sincere, on the other, hand didn't feel comfortable meeting her alone in her personal vehicle. Sincere finally agreed to meet her in one of her friend's vehicles. They linked back up together and it was like old times; she promised Sincere she would never leave again or stay away from her. As a surprise she had reserved a room at the Canterbury Suites for a brief encounter, or so Sincere thought. However, once in the room Sincere noticed a separate set of keys on the counter. Sincere looked around the room, then she found what she feared the most: Chance. He was in the adjoining room, placing rose petals in the hot tub. Sincere instantly became very nervous and ill all at the same time. Not wanting to go down this road with either of them in any form, she turned and dashed for the door feeling like this was a true setup or trap of some sort.

Chance rushed to the door and pleaded for her to stay. Chance appeared defeated and broken as he spoke to Sincere. "If this will allow my wife to stay at home and not divorce, then I am all for it!" Sincere felt betrayed. She looked over at Michelle as if to say *bitch you should have told me!* Michelle's face no longer wore the beautiful comforting smile; it now showed confusion and a need for reassurance. Her eyes pleaded for Sincere to stay without her mouth ever opening. Sincere felt conflicted on whether she would leave or stay. She hesitated for a moment, then agreed. Chance allowed them all the time they wanted to be alone without any interaction from him. They both figured he wasn't happy, considering he broke every single hanger in the hotel room. Choosing to ignore the brewing eruption in the other room, Michelle laid back as Sincere began to kiss her in plain view of the camera Chance had set up in the corner.

Not sure how long she would be able to see Michelle or how long this encounter would be, she put on her best performance. Michelle was midstream in the middle of a serious orgasm when Chance burst in the room with a scowl on his face. He snarled at Sincere while walking towards the camera. "Don't mind me ladies. By all means, continue," he chuckled as he proceeded toward the door.

Both women paused as a sudden uneasy feeling seemed to have entered the room when Chance walked out. Michelle sat up in the bed unable to concentrate any longer. Sincere simply froze, not sure whether to leave or stay. She opened her mouth unable to speak; words were nowhere near the point of exiting her mouth, as if they were just as scared as she was. Suddenly she leaped to her feet and began pacing back and forth, thinking of a way to exit altogether. Heading in the direction of the camera to grab her clothes, she realized her cell phone and clothes were all missing. "Michelle, where in the hell is my cell phone!" she demanded. Sincere knew she left it on the counter by the camera, and apparently Chance had taken them when he came in messing with the camera. Now she had no choice but to leave the room with Michelle; she needed her phone.

As Sincere opened the door, she noticed the room Chance was sitting in was completely clean, as if he knew they were finished when he came in the room. Both sets of clothes were neatly folded on the table with their cell phones sitting right on top. Sincere quickly grabbed her stuff, dressed and left without so much as a good bye, which was a first. Sincere was far from a dummy; she knew when enough was enough. She felt bad leaving Michelle there to deal with Chance, but she had to follow her gut this time. As she drove out of the parking lot, Brenda called to see how she was doing since she hadn't returned any of the text messages she had sent the night before. Sincere looked puzzled, not sure what she was talking about. She hadn't got any messages from Brenda, or anyone for that matter.

Chance's revenge

Immediately after Sincere left, Chance began to beat Michelle once she was out of out of clear view. He never uttered a word as he struck her continuously in various parts of her body. He was always careful never to strike her in the face, as he didn't want their kids to ever see bruises on her. This beating, in Michelle's mind, was the worst ever because he had set everything up, down to arranging the room for them to go to.

Chance looked at his wife now cowering in the corner, trying to hide from being hit again. Chance walked over to help her up. He began to plead with her as to how much he loved her and doesn't want to ruin their family by this fling she was determined to keep having with Sincere. He sat next to Michelle on the bed and began kissing her passionately. She was unfazed by the advances, but she knew she better go along or he may just beat her again. He undressed Michelle to enter her from behind. While stroking his hardening manhood, he stopped when he saw the countless bruises he had placed on her back and arms.

No longer in the mood, he began to cry and apologized to Michelle for hurting her.

Tears and rage built up in her as she put a plan together to leave in the next two weeks, taking Sincere with her. Michelle was in deep thought as Chance's pleas went unanswered. He knew how to get her attention for sure. He decided against striking her, so he rose from the bed, bearing all nine inches right in her face. He grabbed Michelle by the back of her head. She slowly opened her mouth to take him in. She decided against biting him and began to take all of him into her mouth slowly.

Michelle thought of Sincere as she licked, sucked and pulled on his manhood. He felt the difference in her touch, but he was about to unload and didn't want to let thoughts of Sincere kill his vibe. Chance was building up for a massive explosion when he thought, what better way to degrade a woman than to disgrace her by shooting all over her face. Chance softly spoke to Michelle,

"That's right baby, keep thinking I'm her. Oh yeah, baby, just like that!"

As she braced herself for his milk to flow directly down her throat, Chance abruptly pulled his pole from her mouth, allowing it to fall all over her face.

Michelle was mortified, although she didn't let her anger or disgust show; instead, she rose from the bed and cleaned herself up. She waited in the car as Chance entered the hotel lobby, holding the videotape hostage in his pocket. Michelle was franticly searching for the tape when Chance got back in the car laughing. Michelle asked,

"What's so damn funny?"

"I saw you looking for the tape of you and your bitch, huh!"

Michelle sat back quietly in her seat with her arms folded across her chest. He tapped his shirt pocket and said,

"Naw baby, this is evidence, baby! I got just what I need. If you ever think of leaving me for that bitch, I will show this to our kids. I will tell them you choose pussy over them. I will make sure they fucking hate you!"

Michelle cried uncontrollably, now even more determined to leave in two weeks with Sincere by her side. Michelle pulled out her phone to text Sincere and was amazed to find every single text message and picture of Sincere was removed from her phone. She didn't dare ask Chance what happened because it may have been a far worse beating than earlier that day. Chance watched Michelle from the corner of his eye. He knew she was looking through her phone and said,

"Oh yeah, I erased her from the phone, and if she so much as calls I will make her disappear altogether!" Michelle sat quietly as Chance began screaming and yelling about Sincere tearing their family apart.

After Sincere ended her call with Brenda while driving back to the Bay Area, she was reliving the night with Michelle and that odd feeling about Chance. She scrolled through her cell wondering why Michelle hadn't called or texted her yet. While sitting at the longest light in Babcock County and still scrolling, she realized Chance deleted everything in her phone regarding Michelle. She couldn't believe this nigga was being so damn petty over some shit he initiated just because he couldn't participate. What the hell?

Monday morning...

Michelle went to the office early the following morning as if everything was fine between her and Chance. She even sexed him really good the night before to make it so she could leave the house without incident when it came time for work. Luckily for Michelle and Sincere, Chance had no idea Sincere worked for the firm under Michelle.

They both must have been on the same wavelength as they seemed to have emailed each other at the very same time. Sincere smiled as she read Michelle's invite to lunch to discuss something. Sincere managed to pull up in a different car and watched the area before making her way to the meeting location. Michelle stared out of the window, unaware Sincere had even walked in. Michelle immediately began crying when she smelled Sincere's signature fragrance, Michael Kors by Michael Kors.

The plan to leave

They ate lunch and made idle small talk when Michelle dropped a bomb on Sincere. Michelle began to cry as she spoke, "Sincere, I can't take it anymore, it's time!"

Sincere was unsure as to what to say or do, besides just looking extremely puzzled; she waited for Michelle to explain herself. Michelle went on to explain her thoughts and plans. Michelle told Sincere it was time for her to leave Chance and the kids after this weekend; she couldn't stay there anymore. She continued to listen as Michelle went over the details of the beating, the sex episode, him wiping their phones clean, and the final straw was him threatening to remove Sincere from existence altogether. She also revealed his threats to turn the kids against her with the video of the two of them having sex. Sincere sat in shock as she listened to the words flow from her friend's mouth. Michelle asked her to go away with her so that Chance couldn't stop them from being together. Sincere selfishly began to wonder about her own children. What about her job, her house? Her life was now in the Bay Area.

Sincere willingly agreed to leave the day after Labor Day with her with to a destination unknown.

For the first time in a long time things seemed to be in a complete blur for Sincere; she literally had no plan. She was truly stepping out in the name of love for this woman…or was it out of pure stupidity? She had to be crazy, she thought to herself. Who's to say this was real? And, most importantly, that this nigga won't try to find or follow them? Chance was crazy enough to kill both of them. He fit the profile. If he couldn't have Michelle, then no one could! Michelle finally began to smile and seemed to feel a sense of relief knowing Sincere would be by her side within the next two weeks for good. She gave specific instructions to follow when putting in her two week notice with the firm. No loose ends were allowed. Michelle proceeded to put in her notice when she walked back to her office. They both agreed to only communicate via work email and phone to make it appear Michelle was going along with Chance's wishes of officially being done with Sincere.

The following weekend Sincere placed her stuff in storage and moved herself and her children in with her friend Keisha. Keisha and Sincere were good friends and had never crossed the friendship line. Not to say the curiosity wasn't there on her part, though. Sincere was very grateful Keisha allowed them to stay for the next two weeks or so. Sincere made plans for her kids to stay with her mother when they left the area until they got everything settled. At times she grew restless, unable to speak to Michelle; little did she know Keisha would soon attempt to fill the void.

Michelle grew suspicious of Sincere staying with Keisha when she discovered, after being able to break free and sneak over to see her, they are always in the same room and bed. She was always friendly when Michelle came over, and that pissed Michelle off even more. Keisha was eavesdropping and overheard Michelle and Sincere in the bedroom and grew even more curious about what one woman could do to another woman that sounded that intriguing.

When Sincere walked Michelle out to her car, she felt Keisha staring at them through the curtains in the living room. Keisha couldn't help wondering what the big hype was, though she wouldn't dare mention it to Sincere when she entered the house after walking Michelle out.

Keisha was still in deep thought, talking out loud as Sincere closed the front door. *What in the hell could one woman do to another that a man can't do?* She made a mental note to ask Sincere tonight after Michelle's nightly call when the kids were all asleep. She sucked on her bottom lip at the thought of Sincere giving her the same attention she gave Michelle, even if just to experience it once; she had no idea Sincere was standing right behind her.

Sincere whispered, "Come in the bedroom for a sec." Keisha complied. She already knew what the look was all about, but rather than feel like the aggressor she allowed her to make the first move. Keisha started the conversation on how she hoped Sincere was making the right decision by leaving everything behind to be with Michelle. Sincere listened and appreciated her friend looking out for her. Keisha opened her arms for a hug, then planted a friendly kiss on Sincere's on the cheek. Before anything else could take place, the phone rang.

Keisha

Keisha answered her phone with more attitude than Sincere had ever seen her have throughout their entire ten year friendship. She never even so much as raised her voice at her children when she really should have beat their asses. She walked to the other side of the room, still obviously pissed from being interrupted.

Sincere left the room to give Keisha some privacy. Keisha's call carried on for well over an hour, and by this time Sincere was getting sleepy. She knocked to see if she could at least take a shower then lay down. Keisha nodded for her to come back in. As Sincere walked in the room she could feel Keisha staring at her instead of paying attention to her call. Sincere hoped after her shower that Keisha would be done with her call. Sincere was just finishing up her shower when Keisha ended her call and headed to the bathroom. Keisha was trying to catch a glimpse of Sincere naked. "Damn," Keisha said to herself seeing Sincere out of the shower and wrapped in a towel. Keisha flashed a devilish grin as she brushed her 38D cup breasts up against her in an attempt to get Sincere's attention. Sincere knew this game all too well, many of the girls played this in college along with the *what if* game.

Sincere just smiled as she exited the restroom and lotioned up before she climbed into bed wearing only a t-shirt. Keisha showered quickly, taking extra care to wash the middle just in case Sincere wanted to try her for a midnight snack. She desperately wanted Sincere to show her but didn't dare ask for fear of rejection.

Keisha walked out of the restroom with only a t-shirt on as well and climbed in the king sized bed on the opposite side of Sincere. Sincere lay watching as Keisha moved closer and closer to her until they were practically adjoined at the hip. Sincere looked over at Keisha's face as if to say, *are you sure this is what you want?*

Keisha didn't get a chance to respond or say a word before her cell phone rang again. Keisha didn't get upset this time; it was Dre, an ex of hers from back in the day. Keisha candidly spoke to him over the phone as if speaking secretly to Sincere. Keisha said, "I want to do something, but I think, better yet, I know it's wrong!" while biting her bottom lip, looking directly at Sincere.

Sincere picked up her cue and began touching Keisha's breasts. Keisha began to shutter and move seductively in the bed, begging for more silently. Sincere moved closer to suck on her breasts. They both slowly began to grind their body against one another's. The call was no longer able to continue, as Keisha told Dre she would talk to him later. Sincere slowly took both of Keisha's breasts in her mouth one at a time, playing with them with her tongue, careful not to miss a single spot. While still kissing her breasts, Sincere pulled Keisha's legs in an upright position as she began to slowly slide her fingers in and out of her protruding wetness. Keisha began to moan softly as Sincere continued to tug on her breasts and finger her increasingly wet lips.

She moved from her breasts to her neck as Keisha became more and more aroused, moaning just above a whisper. Sincere slowly kissed her neck, moving towards her lips. Keisha gladly followed her lead, kissing her back with even more passion. Sincere decided against going in straight for the kill. She wanted to take her time with Keisha. She slowly made her way from her lips down to her breasts, moving down even further to kissing her belly ring, all the way down to the wetness that patiently awaited her.

Keisha jumped as Sincere entered her body softly with her tongue. She began to moan softly while steadily increasing in pitch. Sincere moved around Keisha's nectar, taking in her wetness, making her way towards the hardening clit. Sincere grazed Keisha's clit lightly with her tongue, and Keisha began to flutter with excitement.

She focused more on her clit while grabbing both of her breasts in the process. Keisha's wet nectar began to ooze as Sincere slowly began to finger her again while still sucking on her clit. Keisha's moans were now well above a whisper. To keep their children from waking up, Sincere placed a pillow over Keisha's mouth to muffle the cries. Little good it did; Sincere looked up to cover her face back up when she noticed Keisha was crying real tears. She slowly moved away from her to see what Keisha would do next. She really didn't want to stop but decided it was better for the current situation. Keisha reached out for her and kissed Sincere's lips intensely. Sincere moved back to look at Keisha to make sure she was okay. Keisha, somewhat out of breath, mumbled, "Yes, oh my goodness is that what it's like all the time?" Sincere felt her *wings* begin to take form. Sincere knew she was leaving soon, so she decided to give Keisha the time of her life in round two. After Keisha had reached her second climax, Sincere waited until Keisha had calmed down enough to actually have another go. Sincere initially repeated the scene, then changed the game plan; while sucking her clit, Sincere opted for double penetration with two fingers in her wet walls as well as a finger in her exit-only zone.

Keisha, now really unable to control her cum and cries, began to squirt everywhere. Sincere was now satisfied with the outcome. Mission accomplished! Sincere cleaned her up and they both went to sleep.

The next morning was worse than the first encounter with Michelle and Chance. Keisha had become Sincere, while Sincere was behaving like Michelle in the beginning. Sincere was fine with what had taken place, but Keisha was a different story. They both dressed in complete silence and went to their separate offices. Keisha was feeling some sort of way about sleeping with Sincere and decided to be the first to break the silence and sent her an email. Her initial email was a mild blow to Sincere. The email started out with the usual *hello* and *good morning*, nothing else. Then she followed up with another email immediately, saying she wished they hadn't crossed that line but it was great and would love to do it again. She knew Sincere was pretty much spoken for but wished it was different. Michelle didn't deserve Sincere or anyone good, but the wrong ones always got the good ones. Sincere responded assuring her it would be their little secret, and it would take place again that night, so get some rest after work!

Time to talk

Michelle must have been in the fight of her life with Chance the night before. Sincere hadn't so much as gotten a *good morning, Babe* call or one of her *143* emails. Michelle would always say *143*, instead of *I love you,* like it was their secret code. By midmorning, Sincere began to panic when it was well past 10 a.m. and Michelle had not yet contacted her. Sincere found herself watching her email, her cell phone and the clock on the wall as she waited to hear from Michelle. As the clock struck 11:42 a.m. there was still no word from Michelle. Sincere began to shut everything down and got ready to go out in the world looking for her when they bumped into each other on the elevator.

Michelle was a mess. Her hair looked like she had been in a fight with all the wrong combs and lost. Sincere pulled Michelle into her office and closed the door. She was now staring directly at Michelle's face, and under the direct light she noticed the botch job she made at attempting to cover up a black eye. Sincere became enraged, demanding to know what had happened to her, even though she already knew it was no one but Chance. Nothing could have prepared her for what Michelle said next. Michelle looked at Sincere with tears streaming down her face and said she had all of her stuff packed and she was leaving today, right now! Michelle gave her one hour to get her stuff and say good bye to her kids or she would be leaving without her.

Sincere stepped away from Michelle with tears in her eyes, unsure if she had heard her correctly. They said their temporary good byes and decided to meet up at the Quickie Mart outside of town just in case Chance was looking for her. As she ran to her car to call her mother, she anguished over what or how to tell her mother.

Her mother, Sandra, must have sensed something was wrong; she never answers the phone on the first ring. "What's wrong Sincere?" Sandra asked instead of saying hello. Sincere began to cry hysterically, yet she managed to ask her mom to take her children earlier than discussed. Sandra, not wanting to hear her daughter cry, agreed but really didn't want to have to raise her grandchildren. She only wanted them out of the shit that could possibly take place if Chance caught up with them.

Sandra prepared for the children to come stay with her and put a plan together for them to stay with her for good. Once she had the kids in her custody, she planned to call DCS and report the children as abandoned. Sincere ended the call with her mom as she ran in to Keisha's house to quickly gather up her things so Michelle didn't leave without her or change her mind. Now was her big chance; she had foolishly waited years for her to decide to leave Chance, and she wasn't going to blow it by taking too long getting ready.

Finally all packed up, she raced to her children's school to tell them she was leaving and Grandma would be keeping them until she came back to get them in a few weeks. Jay began to cry in her arms as Chyna looked on in disbelief. Sincere was full of emotions. She felt selfish and heartbroken, yet she still decided to leave anyway.

They both arrived at the meeting spot at the same time. Michelle jumped out of her car and hurriedly threw her belongings into the back of Sincere's SUV. After everything was loaded up, they filled the SUV up with gas and headed in the opposite direction. No exact destination in mind. They merely just drove down the highway heading east.

They each had numerous emotions going through them as they drove in complete silence. The drive through the mountains was also strained yet exciting at the same time. When they weren't sitting in complete silence, they took the opportunity to discuss their future. They both had cleaned out their personal accounts back home. Michelle paid all of the monthly expenses from their joint account, leaving him a good month's worth of expenses to carry him and their children. She only took her payroll check since it was the smallest.

They both hoped they made the best decision as they headed off to start their new life together. After driving for several hours, it was now nightfall and Sincere was no longer able to pry her eyes open. She exited the highway and checked into a Ramada Inn directly off the interstate. Once in the room they behaved like two complete strangers unable to be seen in the nude by one another. After all the years of waiting to have Michelle all to herself, she finally had her, and she was scared shitless. Deep down she wanted it to be done differently, but she knew this was how Michelle wanted things done.

Sincere wanted her more than anything in the world at this moment, but her body was not in agreement. They both decided to call it a night so they could head out early in the morning to beat the rush hour traffic.

They spoke briefly before enjoying their alone time in bed together. Today was the first time Sincere could say she felt really free to make love to her without limitations, and she enjoyed every minute of it.

The drive through the mountains seemed to never end as they went up and down, up and down for hours. Michelle started relaxing and laid back in her seat. Sincere looked over at her and caught a glimpse of her right breast. Michelle felt her staring and removed her shirt, whispering, "Come here now." Sincere frantically searched for the nearest rest spot so she could suck and kiss on her breasts, maybe even slide her tongue in between her legs briefly. "Shit!" Sincere yelled as she passed a sign on the highway indicating the nearest rest spot was 12 miles away.

Michelle had now climbed in the back seat to remove her clothes. Sincere floored the gas, racing to the exit. Pulling off the exit, Sincere looked in the rear view mirror and found Michelle vigorously fingering herself and rubbing her breasts with her eyes closed. Sincere didn't dare disturb her as the scene was already very nice as it was.

Michelle slowly spread her legs wide enough to perfectly expose her now hardening clit.

She could see her swelling clit pulsate as Michelle's back began to tighten and arch perfectly. Michelle's moaning was beginning to be heard over the music in the car as she continued to please herself.

Sincere knew Michelle was going to cum any minute and hoped she would get the opportunity to fix the wetness she had formed herself. When Michelle was finished pleasing herself, she laid Sincere back and began to undress her. Michelle was amazed to see just how wet Sincere had gotten from watching her. She slid her fingers in Sincere's soaking wet nectar then licked them as she pulled them out of her. Sincere was now seeing a different side to Michelle, and this one she liked a lot. She always hoped Michelle had a hidden freaky side like Brenda, and from the looks of it this was just the beginning. Smiling from ear to ear, they rested for a bit and mapped out their new destination.

As they pulled back on the highway, Michelle's cell phone began ringing nonstop; it was Chance. Michelle refused to answer any of his calls, so he began blowing up Sincere's. Michelle begged her not to answer it. Once he stopped calling them they turned their phones off and changed direction again just in case he was trying to track them through GPS.

As the night approached they settled on the first extended stay they came across in a well-established business district and began to unload their clothes from the truck. Sincere had forgotten just how tired a person becomes when they drive on the highway for extended periods of time. Once everything was unloaded in the room, she was too tired to take a shower or even eat. Michelle seductively removed her clothes, now relaxed and horny as hell. Sincere pulled together all of the energy she could muster up to give Michelle what she needed. They both crashed without eating or showering. The blankets were wet from sweat and other bodily fluids, but they didn't care. They were finally together and that was all that mattered.

New City equals new job

Up and at it, Michelle fixed a light breakfast consisting of coffee and store-bought doughnuts. Sincere couldn't have cared less what she had to eat because Michelle was still there in the morning. They both dressed and left the apartment on a mission to find jobs that day to keep them from depleting their savings in less than a month.

Going door-to-door in lower Manhattan proved to be more of a task than they ever bargined for. They met several different people as they walked up and down the street; some invited them to parties or out on dates. One guy stood out like a sore thumb as he walked up to Michelle wearing Timberland boots and shorts, asking her for her number and out to dinner. She laughed it off, then introduced Sincere as her wife. He took a few steps back and said, "Well damn, can I hang with both of y'all tonight? My treat!" Sincere declined for both of them and took her "wife" by the hand and laughed silently to herself as they walked away from him.

Now headed back to the apartment, Michelle noticed Chance had left several voice mails and text messages on both of their phones. Sincere left her to listen to the voicemails in private. Michelle began to cry in the other room; Sincere ran to see what was the matter, and judging by the look on her face it wasn't good. Sincere asked Michelle what was wrong.

Michelle paused in between each word. Sincere gathered the calls were from their children, mainly Tyler and Christa. CJ wasn't really concerned; she had left them before! Michelle, finally able to speak, fell crying in Sincere's arms as she muttered, "My children hate me! He showed them the video of me having sex with you at the house the first time and also at the hotel."

Sincere couldn't get past this nigga showing children a tape of their mother having sex with a woman; that was a low blow, even for his dog ass. Talk about, if I can't have you, then you won't have our kids either.

"When did he tape us the first time? The camera was never on until he went to work the next morning!"

Michelle, no longer crying, screamed:

"The whole house had cameras in every part of the house recording at all times. How do you think I knew you weren't really asleep when you were at my house the first time we were together?"

Sincere wasn't sure if she should be more mad that Michelle tricked her, or at him for showing the kids her naked ass sucking on her. Michelle played the last voicemail from Chance saying, "If you don't come home on the next plane leaving Friday afternoon, you will have to explain to our kids why I killed myself!"

Suddenly, a loud *bang*, blared through the phone, followed by heavy breathing, a faint gurgling sound, and then silence. Michelle began screaming and running around like Whoopi Goldberg in The Color Purple trying to leave with Shug Avery. Sincere didn't know what she could do to try to comfort her. Michelle was fucking hysterical. Sincere called the local police department for a welfare check and advised them of the possible suicide or attempted suicide. Sincere also told them about the gunshot they heard over the voicemail and advised the dispatcher he may be hurt.

Michelle called Lindell, her mother in-law, to go check on the children. Michelle was relieved to find out the children were already at her house for the next few days, which meant Chance was all alone in the house, possibly dead. Michelle fell to the floor screaming,

"What have I done?" Sincere took a father away from his children because she loved their mother. Sincere had been around these children since they were first born. She was known as Auntie Sin; they would now grow up hating her for sure.

Sergeant Branson from the Bay Area Sheriff's Department called Sincere back when he arrived at the residence, saying Chance was not in the home but there were several bullet holes in the walls. Sergeant Branson then asked for Chance's cell number to have him come back to the house to speak with him regarding the firing of the weapons in the home where minor child reside.

With Chance now wanted for questioning by the police for possible child endangerment, this was way more than Sincere had signed up for. Sincere took this time to take a ride to the mini mart to call her own children in peace without making Michelle feel bad. Chance would never let her speak to them when she called. He always told her they were mad at her or they weren't there. When in actuality they were crying to talk to her, and he comforted them by showing them a video titled, *Your Mommy Chose Pussy over Motherhood!*

Pulling in the mini mart, Sincere called her mother to let her know she was doing okay. No answer, *hmmmm*. She hung up and called back; her mother answered the phone and said she couldn't talk now, that Child Proctection Services (CPS) was there to talk to her about Sincere's kids, and slammed the phone down. What the hell did she mean CPS was there about her children? Sincere didn't understand; she was on the phone calling her, why would she hang up? She called back-to-back nonstop for a full hour before her mother apparently unplugged her phone. Sincere sat in the parking lot trying to reach someone at the CPS office to see what was going on. After being transferred from person to person, Sincere was finally put through to the worker that had just left her mom's house. She introduced herself, then asked about her children and why she was there regarding her children.

Sincere knew it wasn't the worker's job to bond with the parent, but to work in the child's best interest. However, this bitch had an attitude that indicated she needed to get some dick in her life before she took her next breath. No one should be that unpleasant, especially when she was the one calling her.

The worker introduced herself as Mrs. Martinez-Boyd, and she was responding to a child abandonment call. Sincere asked who the hell reported them as abandoned because she had given temporary custody to her mother while she went out of state to get her personal affairs in order. The CPS worker paused as if she didn't believe Sincere until she told her she was the one calling over and over again when she was at her mother's house earlier. The worker provided Sincere a fax number to send her a copy of the temporary custody order showing the date it was signed and given to her mom.

Sincere sped out of the mini mart parking lot and flew up the stairs to their apartment to find Michelle smoking a blunt on the couch and sitting in the dark. Sincere asked if there were any updates in locating Chance. Michelle replied, yes, he turned himself in, but it was leaning more favorably for him since she left her kids to be with her lesbian lover who had also left her children to move out of state.

Michelle looked up from her blunt to see the tears welling up in Sincere's eyes.

"Hey Sin, whats wrong? Are your kids okay?" she asked with concern in her voice.

Sincere fell to the floor and quickly briefed Michelle on her on the conversation with the CPS worker.

Both of them were now wondering on the inside if they had made the right choice by leaving the way they did. Michelle helped Sincere locate the notarized copy of the temporary order showing it was just signed two days prior. Sincere went back to the mini mart to fax it the CPS worker. The CPS worker was kind enough to let Sincere know she had received it. Ironically, the report was made the same day the kids were given to their grandmother, which struck as odd with the CPS worker. Mrs. Martinez-Boyd paused and said to Sincere, "Off the record, go back and get your kids as soon as you can; your mother was the one who reported them as abandoned!"

Michelle was on the phone talking to her children, telling them she loved them very much and she would be home as soon as she could. Sincere walked in to the tail end of her saying she was going back home, which not only pissed her off to no end but also made her want to hit her as hard as she could in her head. Sincere walked out the room and slammed the door. Was this bitch really talking about leaving? And Sincere had CPS trying to take her children? Was she fucking nuts?

Sincere was so over this wishy-washy- ass bitch, she really didn't care if Michelle left or not at this point.

Between all the CPS bullshit and Michelle's mounting drama, she still managed to land a job interview for the following morning. She needed to get this job just in case Michelle really did leave.

The next morning, Sincere went to her interview and was hired on the spot. Michelle on the other hand was not so lucky job-wise. After Sincere's first job offer, she obtained three more the same day. Michelle began to sink into a mild depression each time she was denied the opportunity to speak to her children. Chance knew she really loved her children and they were the only bargining tool he had left. He and Michelle started talking more and more secretly every day as her need for alcohol had increased also.

Unable to sleep, Sincere woke up to find Michelle on the phone talking to the airline booking a flight and seeing all of her stuff was completely packed up. Chance had won and Sincere just wasn't willing to fight anymore.

Michelle was, after all, his wife, and she owed only him her loyalty, no matter the sacrifices Sincere had made to be there with her. After purchasing her flight for the next day, Michelle had the nerve to ask Sincere if she could take her to the airport on her lunch break.

Back to Chance she goes

Sincere laid next to Michelle sick to her stomach, with tears streaming down her face, for damn near half the night. Hell naw, Sincere was determined she wasn't going to be the one to take her to the airport to go back to him. She looked over at Michelle as she slept next to her. She hated to admit it, but this was the most peaceful she had looked the whole time they had been there. Maybe it was meant for Michelle to go back to her family, and she was just being selfish wanting to keep her all to herself.

Both of their lives seemed be doing a downward spiral. She loved Michelle and really wanted to be with her, but not like this, not with all of the anger and bitterness and children on the verge of being taken away. Sincere decided on getting up and ready for work since she hadn't really slept any at all that night. Michelle wanted marathon sex since she was leaving that afternoon to go back to Mister, as he was now affectionatly referred to.

Hearing the water running, Michelle slid out from underneath the covers in a last-ditch effort to have one more round before Sincere headed out the door. Michelle crept up to the bathroom and slowly opened the door. There stood Sincere naked in the shower unable to stop crying, not realizing she had been the shower so long the hot water was completely gone. Michelle snapped Sincere out of whatever trance she was in and helped her out of the shower. Sincere knew Michelle had left in the past but this time it was different. Sincere had left her children, her house and her job to be with Michelle and this was an utter slap in the face to her. She wasn't even mad at her, naw, fuck that, she was past pissed off at her. Mister would get the last laugh this time for sure at Sincere's expense.

Sincere left the house and drove to work on straight autopilot. Luckily, she made it to the office in one crying piece. She couldn't believe she was this emotional over some pussy, really. She forced herself to pull it together long enough to get in her office to close the door. Sincere avoided the usual coffee and breakroom stop to keep from being seen by anyone until she could make sure she had all her emotions in check. She made it to her office undetected; arriving early had some perks. Glancing at her calendar she began to sink down in her overstuffed office chair. *Who in the hell scheduled me for a conference this morning*? Shit, she was in no condition to be speaking to her collegues about anything, whether it be over the phone or in person.

She wanted to be left alone to wallow in her own sadness and dancing in her own pity party. She hadn't noticed Lisa, her administrative assistant, sitting in her office when she raised up her head. Startled, Sincere asked her how long she had been sitting there. Lisa responded, "Long enough to see you need to not be here trying to work!" Sincere thanked her for the concern and asked what she could do for her. Sincere knew she was hurting over Michelle, but shit, she was still human.

Sincere had never noticed how pretty Lisa was until now. Casual flirting was the last thing she needed to be doing, so she put it on hold and let Lisa do her thing. Women always want what they can't have. Sincere played that card to her advantage. Michelle called her cell repeatedly for an hour; not realizing it was ringing, Sincere didn't answer. Out of concern, Michelle jumped in a cab and headed to Sincere's office. Lisa and Sincere were talking strategies for the upcoming conference when Michelle burst into the office. Lisa glanced at Michelle, then back at Sincere and continued as if she wasn't even in the room. Michelle feeling truly disrespected cleared her throat. Sincere took note of her tone and asked Lisa to give them moment alone. Lisa agreed, gathered her files and took one last long up-and-down glance at Michelle while strutting out of Sincere's office, mumbling. The pissed off side of Sincere was laughing on the inside and telling herself: *see you got another chick right here ready to take this bitch's place since she wants to go back to getting her ass beat on a regular!*

Michelle stood in front of her, still upset about being disrespected by Lisa, and tapped her foot in frustration. Sincere looked away, then asked Michelle what was so important she needed to come to her office and continue to rub in her face the fact that she was leaving. Michelle cleared her throat, lowering her voice to just above whisper, telling Sincere to check her cell. Michelle explained she had been calling her for over an hour to give her the travel plans to leave that afternoon were changed and she was leaving within the hour.

"What? So you really came down here to rub this shit my face some more!" Sincere yelled. Sincere tried desperatly to hold back her tears but it was useless. Tears began to roll down her face, so she let them roll. Lisa burst in Sincere's office to make sure everything was ok. Lisa attempted to comfort Sincere as if Michelle wasn't in the room at all. Michelle was now a distant memory, invisible even! Michelle had taken all she could take from Lisa's disrespectful ass and foricibly removed her hands off Sincere then pushed Lisa out of the office. The look of horror on Michelle's face spoke volumes without her even uttering a word. Sincere sat there in silence. Although Michelle only stood 5 feet 2 inches, weighing a mere 105 pounds, she was a force to be reckoned with if provoked.

Sincere let Michelle know she had a conference coming up and it wasn't going to be possible for her to take her to the airport. Michelle, still obviously pissed about Lisa, dismissed Sincere's response, indicating she was saying goodbye now; she had a cab waiting outside to take her to the airport. Sincere's heart sank lower and lower. *Damn,* Michelle was really going to go through with it.

They embraced one another, neither one wanting to be the first to let go. Lisa knocked on the door to tell them Michelle's cab was blowing the horn in segments. Sincere kissed Michelle goodbye and walked her to the cab for one final goodbye.

"Well, I guess this is it until you return to the Bay Area", Michelle said. Sincere let go of her hand and said,

"I'm not returning to go through this back and forth stuff with you and Mister all over again. This did it for me".

Michelle seemed out of sorts when Sincere said she was staying there.

"How can you stay here without me?" she asked. Sincere, now speaking from hurt, said:

"Easily, just like you packed up and left me here. It's just that easy!"

Sincere's words burned through Michelle like venom. She knew this was making it worse for her to leave. Michelle had a choice and she made it, so it was now for her to live with. Lisa peeked around the doorway wanting to see exactly what was going on. Behind them several of the smokers stopped smoking and were focused solely on them and the running cab. Sincere opened her door and kissed her forehead one last time, then closed the door and walked back toward her office. Lisa took notice of Sincere's tears and was ready to be 'Jane on the Spot' to comfort her later.

Sincere resisted each of her advances, but Lisa was very persistent. Lisa cleared Sincere's calendar and offered to take her home. Sincere respectfully declined! She didn't need to be alone or with someone she was clearly very attracted to. If messing with Brenda taught her nothing else, she learned not to fuck with any coworkers and surely not one of her direct reports. Lisa had an agenda and she was not taking the word *no* very easily. Sincere decided to stay in the office to help take her mind off Michelle leaving her. Drowning herself in work always made stress a little easier to handle.

Michelle arrived at the airport, her mascara running down her face from crying, convincing herself this was best for her children. Hell, CJ was eight, she could deal with Chance another 10 years if he didn't kill her first. She checked in and was making her way to airport security when her phone began to ring.

"Hi, Mommy," blared through the phone. Chance let the children call her before she boarded the plane. Michelle told them how much she missed them and let them know she had a surprise for them.

Chance abruptly cut her off before she could tell them she was coming home. Michelle ignored the fact he was on the line the whole time she spoke to her children while walking through the airport. He instructed the children to hang up the line so he could talk to Mommy; they all complied, excited and screaming, "Mommy's feeling better, she's coming back home to us."

Chance stepped out on the deck to talk to Michelle and give her the new list of rules to returning to *his* house with *his* children. He gave her the rules and made her repeat them:

1. I am to have no contact with Sincere or anyone associated with her.

2. I am only allowed to leave the house when escorted by someone else.

3. I am to work in the house only.

4. I can have no female friends.

Michelle couldn't believe she was agreeing to any of this, but she did and boarded the plane back to her old- but newly controlled-life.

Sincere sat in her office staring at her cell, waiting to get a call from Michelle to let her at least know she made it there okay. Her plane landed hours ago, yet still no word. Sincere spoke the obvious: she's back home and they were back on the *not able to be friends* ride again.

"This shit is bananas! I'm off this ride and off this chick!" she roared out loud. She began shutting down for the day when Lisa entered her office and took a seat, asking how she was now feeling and she hoped she wasn't intruding by being concerned about her. Sincere wasn't sure how she could suddenly care so much about her. She had only been her direct report for less than a week. Sincere thanked her again for the concern today. Glancing at her watch she noticed it was nearly 8 p.m., and Lisa should have been gone at 5 p.m.. Jokingly, Sincere asked if she was still clocked in. Lisa grinned and slyly held up the Girl Scout honor sign replied, "No. I clocked out at 5 p.m., I just live around the corner!"

"Hmmm, is that right?" Sincere shot back

Lisa licked her lips, shaking her head in agreement. Damn, Ray Charles could see where this is headed. Sincere thanked her again and attempted to get past her in a hurry. Lisa jumped to her feet to stop Sincere from walking past her. From the jolt, both of their breasts brushed against one another. Sincere quickly apologized; a sexual harassment suit was the last thing anyone in corporate America needed.

Lisa laughed, "No one's clothes came off, so we're good," she stated.

Damn, Sincere knew she had to get away from this one here; she was testing her for real. Finally out of the building and headed to her truck, she noticed her truck was the only one left in the parking lot and it was completely dark. Sincere turned around to find Lisa was no longer behind her or anywhere in sight for that matter. Either this chick was fucking Houdini or Sincere must be tired and delusional. She stood there talking to herself out of thinking she was crazy. Sincere opened the truck door to put her bag in the back and there sat Lisa in the middle section completely naked. "Oh shit!" Sincere said while wondering how in the fuck Lisa got in her truck or even get past her without seeing her. Lisa's body was very nice and toned. Lisa was a mixed petite-framed woman with green eyes; she was absolutely gorgeous. Even though Sincere vowed not to do women she worked with anymore, she was almost willing to make an exception in this case.

"Shit," she said again out loud before asking Lisa to get dressed so she could head home. Lisa looked mortified when Sincere denied her strong advances yet again. Lisa asked Sincere, "Don't you like what you see or find me attractive?" Instead of trapping herself, Sincere went in supervisor mode and reiterated that fraternizing on the job is grounds for termination and she wasn't taking that chance for a quick roll, regardless of what she thought.

Lisa, still clearly very upset, said she understood then asked for a ride home, which Sincere again declined. She was going through enough without being caught on camera taking a subordinate home after hours in her personal vehicle. Sincere suggested a cab and Lisa accepted. Sincere waited until it arrived. As freaking luck would have it, the same cab driver that brought Michelle to the office earlier that day was the same damn one to take Lisa home. If the walls of his cab could talk, they would be screaming all kinds of shit Sincere's way.

The look on his face was more than enough for Sincere. The driver got out of his vehicle to open the door for Lisa, more to get a closer look at her. Once she was in the car, he walked back past Sincere, giving her the thumbs up. Sincere gave him a look like *man we ain't cool and this is not that!*

Sincere didn't care; fine or not she made sure she was free and clear from any wrongdoing on this night with Lisa. The cab slowly pulled off the lot and headed in the same direction Sincere was going. A coincidence, maybe or maybe not, but Sincere was too exhausted to care, she was just glad she could finally head home.

Who wants Sincere the most?

Driving home from the office, Sincere noticed the cab was still in her sights. Lisa apparently lied about where she lived, but that was her deal, not Sincere's. Sincere turned to get on I-95 so she could beeline to her apartment. As she pulled onto the interstate, she no longer saw the cab so she brushed it off. Turning on her radio, she immediately got sad. The radio blared Ne-Yo's *Make it Work*. Really? At a time like this? "Naw, not tonight," she said, switching to a club banger in her six disc CD changer. Out poured Lil Jon's *Put Yo Hood Up!* Yeah, now this she could roll with, something to turn up her mood. Sincere was grooving to the music when her cell phone rang. It was Keisha; she had just touched down in the area for a getaway and wanted to see Sincere. Sincere got the info where Keisha would be staying at and continued to chat for a bit.

As she pulled into the apartment for what was supposed to be rest, she screamed, "Bullshit!" just as her grandfather used to say when he was being snowballed. Looking at the security gate outside the apartment, *were her eyes deceiving her*? It couldn't be that cab at her damn apartment. Sincere jumped out of the truck, mad as hell this time. Staring at the driver she screamed, "What the hell is up? Why are you following me?"

The driver, obviously not in the mood for a bitch with an attitude, said in a stern tone, "Calm yo little hot headed ass down, ain't nobody following you. I live here too." Not believing him at all, she waited for him to open the gate with his own security code. *Damn*, the gate opened, so she guessed he did live there also. But to make sure, she followed him through the gate. This shit was just too coincidental as he pulled in the garage right next to hers. Shaking her head as she walked through the corridor to get on the elevators, he was hot on her heels. *Fuck*, he was getting in the same elevator as her too with his fine ass.

Looking like Mr. Chestnut, Morris, that is. The elevator stopped and they both got off on level seven taking the same hall. This nigga lived right next door to Sincere! She opened her door as he entered his apartment and locked it behind her. Before she could take a shoe off there was a knock at the door. Suddenly this nigga was feeling neighborly and wanted to have a drink after a hard day. Sincere cut him short and said, "Hey thanks for everything today, but on a serious note I'm good on the neighborly thing!"

Instead of him being offended, he smiled and extended his hand to introduce himself. He said his name was Derek, he knew she was new to the area and now lived alone. He explained he merely wanted to show some hospitality to a seemingly hostile neighbor. They each laughed, which broke the ice. Sincere stopped him in mid-conversation and asked him if they could follow up another day, she had some place she needed to be within the next hour. Derek smiled and said, "Sure, but hey make sure to close your windows if you have company; everyone doesn't need to see you working it out in the bedroom!"

Totally embarrassed, Sincere stopped in her tracks and asked him how often he watched her and Michelle.

"Often enough to know she liked being watched, by me!" he answered.

Well that explained the sudden interest in all the nightly sessions with the curtains drawn back. Derek headed towards the door.

"Just wish I could have gotten with both of you before she left this evening," he mumbled.

136

Sincere corrected him.

"No, she left this morning, and what you mean got with both of us?"

Derek slowly turned to face her.

"Is that what she told you? Okay, well that explains the back-to-back calls to your office today."

Puzzled and intrigued at the same time, Sincere asked him to clarify what he was saying. He went on to say when he was leaving this morning for a jog when Michelle stopped him and asked him to run her to the office for a small cashless fee. *What man is going to turn down sex from a beautiful woman?*

He said he had agreed to bring her to the office and waited outside as he was instructed. Once Michelle went inside, Lisa, the lady he picked up that evening, came out and asked him to be available around 8 p.m. to come back to get her, and she paid him $100 on the spot. Michelle got back in his cab in tears. Derek continued to give her grave details about the ride back to the apartment with Michelle. He explained when they got back to the apartment Michelle told him she had time to do whatever because she knew Sincere wasn't going to leave work. She made a call to someone then said she could change her flight to leave later on; she had confirmed you for sure wouldn't be there for a while, she knew you all too well.

Derek smiled and said, "Apparently she does know you like she said, because we fucked here for several hours before I dropped her off at the airport!" Then he got a text from the Lisa babe at the office to come back.

Damn, Sincere felt stupid as hell! She trusted her but hell she's gone now and Keisha was here waiting for her. What better way to handle frustration, none other than good sex from a willing participant?

Derek let himself out and promised to hold Sincere to the follow-up later on that week. With Derek gone she focused on getting dressed to see Keisha. Michelle fucking Derek earlier that day was on the back burner, let alone her leaving to go back to Mister.

Keisha was a true breath of fresh air after today's events. Sincere needed a true stress reliever as well as a release of newly built up sexual frustration. Keisha was just what any head doctor would have ordered. She could see the script now:

Must give and receive multiple orgasms, PRN.

Signed,

Dr. Feel Good

Sincere laughed to herself as she made her way up to Keisha's suite to unwind. Sincere knocked on the door, but it went unanswered. Sincere checked to make sure she had the right room. Yes, it said room 362, so she was at the right door, so she knocked again; this time Keisha answered that the door was open. Sincere entered the room ready to fuss for having to knock twice. Once inside she decided against when she saw Keisha had prepared a candlelight dinner, followed by the sweet sound of R. Kelly's *Strip for You* in the background.

Shit, this is how you want to be greeted when you enter a room!

Keisha looked absolutely beautiful, her shear gown complimented her frame nicely. Her hair was pulled up in a bun revealing a new tattoo behind her left ear. Sincere walked over and gave her a long hug and proceeded to kiss her softly on her lips. Keisha stepped back and whispered,

"Wait, I have another surprise for you!"

Man, after today Sincere didn't want any more surprises, not right this very moment anyway. Sincere hesitated and said, "Oh, wow you really shouldn't have," as she glanced around the suite and saw no packages, boxes or cards in sight.

Keisha laughed and said stop spinning around before you make yourself sick, it's not out here, it's in the bedroom. Oh yeah, this was steaming up to be Sincere's type of surprise. Sincere took her hand and followed Keisha to the bedroom. The double doors swung open, the bed was covered in red, black and white rose petals in the red candlelit room. She pulled Keisha in her arms to thank her when Keisha said, "One moment babe, there's more!" Sincere's heart was on overload at this moment. What else could there be? Keisha swung her head in the direction of the nightstand. Sincere slowly walked over to the nightstand and grabbed the small envelope, her eyes focused on Keisha as she opened it up. The envelope contained two tickets to Vegas with both their names listed on each ticket. Now that was a great way to end this fucked up day she had.

Keisha was a good pick-me-up and just what Sincere needed. She grabbed Keisha before she had a chance to pull away from her, and Sincere planted a set of serious kisses on her lips as a thank you for all that she had done for her. Keisha, now a bit stunned, stumbled into the other room to unveil the dinner she had prepared for both of them. She retreated to the restroom to wash her hands and noticed the shower was wet. As she washed her hands, she called Keisha in the bedroom as if something was wrong. Keisha flew in the room next to Sincere's side to see what was wrong. Sincere pulled her close and said everything was perfect. Keisha was more worried about the food getting cold in the other room and tried to pull away. Sincere whispered, "The main course is right here," as she began to lift up Keisha's sheer gown to just above the hips. Keisha made her way down to the bed to keep from losing her balance. She was now lying in just the right position for Sincere to go to work on her.

Sincere kept the gown above her waist as she pulled her left thigh to her side, baring her bare ass just the way she liked it. Sincere detested undergarments and soon any woman that interacted with her would learn to not wear them around her also. She began to finger Keisha softly while removing her own clothes slowly.

Keisha was now more comfortable touching Sincere without coercion. She unbuttoned Sincere's blouse so she could suckle her breasts. Sincere's body was in agreement with all of her touches as her own nectar quickly moistened. Beads of sweat were forming on her forehead as Sincere began to suck her toes and softly massage her foot. She motioned for Sincere to kiss her favorite spot. Sincere wasn't ready to get her off just yet as she moved her hands to rest at her side and finished sucking each of her toes one at a time until all ten were tended to.

Moving Keisha's left leg back to the side, Sincere rolled her tongue up the back of her thigh until she reached the lower end of her ass cheeks. Sincere massaged Keisha's ass firmly and wondered if she should blow Keisha's mind by licking around the crevasse or just tease the middle with her fingers. She decided on continuing to lick around the outer and inner crease of her ass while slowly turning her on the left side, since that leg was now back down to her side.

Keisha braced herself for entry at this point, not sure where she was going, as she closed her eyes and exhaled softly. Sincere moved her tongue from the side of her ass to her slightly parted lips, moving about graciously in her wetness while becoming very wet herself. Tonight was about Keisha and only Keisha; Sincere felt she owed her much. Keisha moved seductively to each of her touches, whimpering and begging for more at the same time. Sincere pleased Keisha in ways that went beyond a typical fuck or one-night stand. Keisha pulled her gown over her head, revealing her breasts along with another new tattoo. The tattoo caught Sincere's eye as from a glimpse it seemed to have her name *Sin* smack dab in the middle of a pair of ladies legs.

Damn, she not only wanted to take Sincere to Vegas with her, but she had also tattooed her name on that ass, literally. Once she saw that Keisha was determined, nothing was going to break her duty to make this special for her. She had a genuine love for Keisha, even though they could never have a relationship for the obvious reason, her love for that fucked up ass Michelle.

For tonight, Sincere put thoughts of Michelle, Derek and Lisa totally out of her mind. They finished up in the bedroom with Keisha tossing Sincere's salad; this was a different kind of kink. Sincere loved a freaky woman. The feeling she got from Keisha's backdoor action was amazing until she tried to insert a finger and it was over as fast as it began. Sincere liked lots of things in the bedroom but that was not one of them. Now she was not opposed to it by any means; generally it was her that was the one performing

143

this and not the one on the receiving end of it. Sincere was uncomfortable about it, but once she warmed up to it she got into it and went into straight *bitch mode* when she had a feeling erupt inside her leaving her completely vulnerable when Keisha touched her. Sincere knew she was about to cum when her pitch continued to rise over and over. She was screaming and cumming at the same time.

Shit, is that what it felt like for the women she had done this to? She had to admit she was impressed, Keisha surpassed all truly surpassed all of her expectations. Sincere was full of her juices and, along with being thoroughly exhausted, had no room for the dinner Keisha had prepared. They lay in each other's arms sleeping and dead to the world around them!

Michelle's back home

Chance met Michelle at the airport to make sure she really came home like she promised she would. Michelle, tired from the flight, was in no mood to argue with Chance tonight so she was willing to comply with anything he asked of her. He stood at the gate with flowers and a *Welcome Home* balloon for Michelle. Michelle pulled her sun hat down to hide from the bright lights off the terminal. Between her sunglasses and hat pulled down blocking her view, she literally ran right into him.

Chance, excited to see her, forgot he had flowers for her in his hand and dropped them during the embrace as the balloon went up in the air. Before he could grab the flowers off the floor, several children ran off the terminal to their awaiting loved ones and trampled all over the flowers. He became very angry on the inside thinking about the damaged flowers and who or what Michelle was doing before she got off the plane because she was supposed to come that morning not that evening.

She sensed something was wrong, so she wrapped her arms around him tighter and began telling him how much she missed him and the kids. He grabbed her luggage from the arriving terminal as Michelle called her children. Tyler answered in an uneven tone as if he didn't know who he was speaking too. Once he caught her voice he asked, "Whose number are you calling from? Because your name didn't come up."

Michelle looked down at her phone, puzzled, to make sure she hadn't grabbed the person's phone seated next to her on the plane by mistake. After confirming it was hers, she told Tyler not to mention it to his dad so it wouldn't be a problem when she got home. Tyler agreed to not say anything.

Chance strutted back to where Michelle stood waiting for him. He said, "Come on baby let's go home!" He got in the car, leaving Michelle on the curb. He rolled down the window to see if something was wrong, and she said, "Oh wait, I forgot you don't open the door for me, never mind," and abruptly stopped talking and opened her own door.

Chance was boiling mad on the inside, yet tried desperately to mask it with Michelle now seated in the car as they drove off.

Chance glanced over in her direction and asked why she hadn't put her seatbelt on yet.

"We aren't going that far and pull over right over there," she said, and pointed in the direction of an open field. He complied, though he was confused.

Michelle got out of the car and headed toward the open field. He jumped out of the car and ran to catch up with her, thinking she was trying to leave him again. After he caught up to her he gripped her arm so tight he left his finger impressions embedded in her arm. Michelle turned to face him.

"I want you to fuck me right here!" she said.

He complied! It began to rain yet they continued as if the sun was shining. After they were finished they headed back to the car holding hands, soaking wet and smiling.

He was ecstatic his wife was back and she wanted *him*, not a woman. Michelle attempted to lean over to give him some head during the ride home. After she placed him

147

in her mouth she got sick and began to throw up profusely in the car. Surprisingly, he wasn't upset; he chalked it up to the change in climate. However, Michelle felt Sincere was with someone else loving them the way she used to love her. The happy arrival was taking a turn for the worse, but Michelle was determined to make it good no matter what. They pulled up in front of their house, CJ, Tyler and Christa ran out to greet Michelle. She cried from excitement, even with vomit on her clothes and all; she was ecstatic to see her children.

Chance took her luggage in the house while the kids loved on their mom. Michelle managed to finally get in the house when she was greeted by Chance's twin sister Cadence. Michelle couldn't stand her, but she tolerated her. Cadence got up from the chair.

"So you finally decided to come up from the pussy for some air? Or did you remember you had a family at home?"

Michelle looked at Chance to see if he was going to check Cadence, but he didn't. He took this opportunity to introduce Michelle to her new personal driver, Cadence, who also now lived with them. Michelle was beyond pissed; she wished she stayed in New York with Sincere.

What in the hell had he done? Chance was speaking to her and Michelle had completely zoned out, not hearing him call her name over and over again.

Suddenly Michelle was on the floor as everything went dark. He had knocked her upside her head for ignoring him and leaving them in the first place. Michelle awoke to Cadence undressing her and putting her in some clean pajamas. Michelle snatched away from Cadence to dress herself. Cadence laughed it off and said, "So you don't want me dressing you, but you let that bitch kiss and suck on you, huh?"

Michelle vowed to leave for good and be with Sincere, but she had to figure out how to get her back up there. Michelle called her cell phone company to ask them about the number on her phone when the agent told her the numbers had been changed the morning before due to a nuisance caller at the request of Michelle's husband, Chance. Michelle decided not to get upset about it, this was what she agreed too. Walking through the house she searched for the luggage Chance brought in the house from the airport. Tyler was watching cartoons in the basement when she asked him if he had seen it. Tyler said he saw it yesterday by the door but it's gone now. "Dad burnt it last night after you went to sleep!"

She slowly walked away, tears welling up in her eyes. Chance and Cadence were on the back deck when Michelle came out of the basement. They both glared in her direction, then they started laughing. She knew they were laughing at her. Now on a mission to get the hell out of there for good, she went to her room just staring out the window day in and day out.

"Daddy what's wrong with mommy? Doesn't she like us anymore?" Christa asked Chance.

"Of course she does princess, she just needs to be alone right now. She's coming down with a weird bug that makes her sad all the time!"

"Oh ok, well I hope I don't get it!"

Chance walked up the stairs and closed the bedroom door. He yanked Michelle's lifeless body up from the chair and shook her like a rag doll, screaming at the top of his lungs.

"You need to snap out of this shit Michelle, right now dammit. You are here because you want to be here with us, your family!"

150

Michelle, weak from not eating over the past several days, whispered,

"Death can't be much worse than being married to you as a prisoner in this house."

He was about to strike her once again when Cadence burst through the door, grabbing his arm before he was able to hit her for speaking to him like that. Cadence told him to leave her alone, it was worse than she thought. Chance said, "Since you know what's wrong with her, fix it so we can get past this shit!"

Cadence looked him in his eyes and said, "I'm sorry, but you have lost her. She's heartbroken, she misses Sincere and you hitting on her is only tiring you out and causing her to withdraw even more!"

Chance put Michelle down then stormed out of the bedroom, slamming the door behind him.

Chance needs Sincere

Chance felt totally defeated as he resorted to calling Sincere to see if she could help Michelle. Whose number is calling from the Bay Area, she wondered. Like most people, if it wasn't listed in her contacts she ignored the call, sending it to voice mail. If the call was important they would leave a message. Whoever it was left a message then called right back, leaving another message. She waited to see if they would call again or leave another message but they didn't. She dialed her voicemail to listen to the messages; it was the fucking bastard Chance calling her. The messages from him sounded desperate, but hell, he's a desperate-ass nigga that couldn't control his wife.

Sincere bypassed the first message of him rambling, then the next one was him saying she's really sad, sick and won't eat, she just stares out the window all day. That wasn't the Michelle she knew and loved at one point. Who was Sincere kidding, Michelle was never her Michelle. Michelle was his and Sincere had been played like a used fiddle for the last time. He pleaded through each message to please at least call back so Sincere could speak to Michelle under his direction.

After being away from their drama-filled lives, Sincere finally started to feel complete, and here he was trying to drag her back down before her trip to Vegas with Keisha. Sincere had finally found the courage to do something she had never done before. Message deleted!

Sincere finished up her work early and waited for Keisha to come grab her so they weren't taking two cars to the airport. Keisha pulled up right on time with a disturbed look on her face. Sincere asked, "What's wrong babe?" with concern in her voice. Keisha looked at her, then passed Sincere a piece of paper on cab company letterhead. Sincere read the message quietly:

Michelle was rushed to the hospital, please call Chance.

"Not my business anymore." Sincere told Keisha, "Let's go babe, we have a flight to Vegas to catch."

Relief filled Keisha's face. Keisha had been by Sincere's side since Michelle left her nearly three months ago and they were going strong. Sincere refused to let anything or anyone bring her back to the low level she had reached when she shed tears over that bitch that played her.

153

The same bitch that left her alone in New York to return to a man that beat on her. "Fuck her and him, good riddance," she mumbled under her breath, planting a few quick kisses on Keisha.

Thank goodness for valet parking or they would have missed the check-in. Keisha had thought of everything. As Sincere rushed over to the check-in line, Keisha went to have a seat. Sincere told her to come on or they would have to board the plane last. Keisha just grinned shyly and said she had already checked them in earlier and they will be the first to board. All right now, just what Sincere wanted to hear at that moment. "Now boarding 001-045," the speakers repeated over and over.

Sincere grabbed Keisha's hand, kissing her own hand softly. "Let's hit it," she whispered as Keisha playfully pushed her blushing face under her wool cap. It was a whopping 21 degrees in New York, and she wore flip flops. Only Keisha could pull off such things. They boarded the plane and took their seats.

Chance continued to call Sincere repeatedly with each call going unanswered. He left so many messages, he filled up her voicemail. Furious now, he paced back and forth, and he wondered why Sincere was ignoring him. He even called her from Michelle's phone hoping she would answer, yet the calls still went to voicemail, which was unable to accept messages, and dropped off.

He stormed in the room where Michelle was being looked over by several doctors. As he entered the room, Michelle's blood pressure began to rise quickly. A medical student observing took notice of her changes and whispered to the doctor what he had noticed. The staff doctor halted Chance in his strut to her bedside and took him outside to speak with him. He proceeded to tell Chance that Michelle was not in a position to have any visitors at the moment. The doctor explained they were trying to stabilize her and keep her as calm as possible to see how her body responded to the new medication. Chance responded angrily.

"What the fuck do you mean she can't have any visitors? I'm her fucking husband, not the janitor. All right cool, no visitors, huh, remember that shit when it's time to pay this muthafuckin' bill!"

He stormed away from the doctor; he knocked over everything in his sight that wasn't bolted to the ground. As Chance neared the elevators he was abruptly met by several security guards. He quickly changed his tone, "I'm cool, I'm leaving, this shit ain't even necessary," he repeated over and over again as he was escorted off the property.

The first guard advised Chance he was now on the no trespassing list until his wife was discharged and was not to come within 50 feet of the hospital grounds. The guards watched as Chance got in his car and sped off the parking lot before they walked back toward the hospital.

"What the fuck!" he screamed as he drove to his parents' house to give them an update on Michelle. Now he'd never know when that bitch Sincere would make her way to the hospital to see Michelle. Where in the fuck was she and why ain't she answering her damn phone?

Aw yeah, he thought of a way to get off that list and back in the hospital. Chance knew she wasn't going to stay away for too long. She must be with another bitch or something, he thought to himself as he pulled out his cell and called the nurse station to work his magic.

"Psych Ward, Nurse Patton, how may I help you?"

"Hey there beautiful how you doing? It's me, Chance."

"Well hello, Mr. Attitude," she responded, "what can I do for you?" Smiling now, Chance replied that he could think of a number of things, but he's a patient man.

"Is that right? Ummm, well I don't have all day; know what I want?" Not expecting that response, he chuckled.

"Now what would that be, Ms. Lady?"

"Well, nothing major, I just want some dick. Can you accommodate me?" .

"I'm sure I can do that and some," he replied. Not wanting to go too far off course, he let her know he would need something in return as well. "Anything for you. What is it?" she asked.

He repeated the earlier events that day where he lost his cool and was now on the no trespassing list. He told her needed to be off that list and a phone call when a certain female comes to see his soon-to-be ex-wife.

"Can you handle all that, Ms. Lady?"

"Is that all? I can do all that and some," she replied quickly. "What's the lady's name?"

"Sincere James," he muttered with an attitude.

"Hm, you seem a bit frustrated about her, baby, is everything ok? If it's none of my business I understand that as well baby," she replied.

"Well, Ms. Lady, it's a long story, but let's just say she's the reason as to why we're getting a divorce once the wife is in better health."

"Oh, I get it, a threesome gone wrong huh? The wife must have fell for her, happens all the time. Don't worry baby, it's all good! Well you're off the list already and I'm down to fuck whenever you are."

Disregarding her comment, Chance thanked her.

"Be ready in an hour since I'm off the list. I wanna fuck you there on the roof!"

"Okay, I'll be ready and waiting," she replied.

"Cool." They both hung up simultaneously.

Two hours later Chance arrived back at the hospital, ready to peek in on Michelle and get with the nurse. As he walked up to the door he was greeted by two of the previous guards from earlier that day that had previously escorted him out of the building.

"Well sir, we see you don't listen very well," stated the first guard.

"Naw, check your book man, I've been taken off the list," Chance replied. The second guard nodded.

"He's good, it says 'Administrative override.' You're free to go with our apologies, sir!"

He smiled as he nodded and strolled past them to the elevators. As the elevator doors opened to the nurse's station on the floor, he noticed the entire floor was clear of any staff members. He could hear voices laughing in the background, though they were distant. He followed the voices until he saw a nurse and several doctors looking on the computer and pointing. Clearing his throat, they all turned in his direction.

"We're very sorry sir, we didn't see you," replied one of the nursing students.

"Yes ma'am it's ok, I'm just looking for Nurse Patton," he replied.

"Oh, okay she went for a break with another nurse; they may be on the roof," she snickered as she quickly walked away.

Heading towards the roof, Chance wondered what the snickering was all about as he headed towards the sign marked ROOF ACCESS. "Damn, this elevator is taking forever," he said out loud as he headed for the stairs.

Finally on the roof after seven flights of stairs, he

noticed the roof access door was jimmied open with a brick. Ok, he thought, she must be up here waiting for me. As he opened the door, he saw two nurses kissing each other heavily. Dammit, not another bitch that likes bitches, he thought to himself.

Nurse Patton opened her eyes to find him staring at her and the other nurse with her head now buried deep in between her legs.

"Oh daddy, I tried to wait as long as I could baby, but I thought you weren't going to come so I had to improvise," she said, trying to catch her breath. "Well shit, since you are here, come here and fill up this extra hole that needs some filling," she said, opening her mouth as wide as she could get it.

Chance walked over and unbuttoned his jeans and pulled out his now hardening dick and plowed it deep in the back of her throat.

Apparently this Nurse Patton was a pro; she didn't gag or spit, she merely repositioned her sucking and pulling on his manhood. He moved around in her mouth well until he felt his eruption brewing and quickly pulled it out. Glancing between the two nurses he decided on fucking

Nurse Patton, as she was now licking the other nurse from behind. Chance grabbed her by the hips and firmly squeezed as he moved in and out with strong thrusts. Nurse Patton seemingly enjoyed rough sex with both men and women. Chance, still not ready to cum, stopped pumping as he pulled his manhood out, now demanded they switch so he can plow the younger nurse in her ass.

The younger nurse was shy and reluctant to have him fuck her in her ass. With a little persuasion from Nurse Patton she finally gave in and awaited his entry. Chance dropped large amounts of spit from his mouth directly in her ass as he inserted one finger at a time until he had three fingers in her ass comfortably. He pulled his fingers out and placed his hard dick roughly in her ass. Forcing his fingers in her wet lips and moved them about slowly as the nurse whimpered and begged for mercy. He must have zoned out as he began to wildly move his dick in and out of her ass while fucking her harder and harder. The nurse began to buck like a wild boar. She didn't know whether to cry or scream as she began to cum from all now sorely occupied areas of her body at the same time.

Nurse Patton sat back on the ledge no longer part of this experience, and rubbed her breasts and clit for her own gratification. She seemed to enjoy watching more than the any of the sexual acts she had received on her own. Chance now felt satisfied decided to finish off the younger nurse with getting his dick sucked one last time. She cowered on her knees and took him into her mouth and sucked his manhood while rubbing his sweaty balls. She fought hard not to gag, considering his dick was just in her ass and the other nurse's mouth only moments earlier.

Chance's dick was growing harder and harder in her mouth, yet she continued. Chance knew he was about to cum, so he grabbed the back of her head to hold her still. The younger nurse was not into swallowing so she tried to pull away from his grip. As the explosion started, he pulled out and sprayed his cum all over her face. Chance shook his dick violently to get it all out. With his balls now completely empty he placed his throbbing, limp dick back in his jeans and walked away saying, "Thank you ladies, it's been real, yes, a real pleasure indeed!" Both nurses where horrified and equally embarrassed at the treatment. They both quickly dressed and vowed to never tell anyone how they got played!

Land over Air any day

All the turbulence from the plane had made Keisha a basket case. The slightest movement made her throw up terribly. While they walked through the airport Sincere checked her phone. Damn, 16 missed calls from what appeared to be Chance, along with countless text messages. Keisha looked over toward Sincere and said, "It's okay babe, check your messages. I'll get the valet and gather our bags!"

Sincere kissed her and told her how lucky she was to have her in her life, Keisha's smile was thanks enough. Sincere sat in the designated cell area and began to check her slew of messages. Messages one to fifteen were all Chance wanting her to call him back.

15 messages were deleted. Press number1 to confirm.

Sincere quickly pressed 1.

"You have one new voicemail."

This number was different; it was a man's voice, though she had no idea who Dr. Philpot was. Then it dawned on her, Michelle must really be in the hospital. Fuck, she had deleted all the other messages from Chance, so Sincere had no idea what was really going on. Sincere listened to the doctor's message; he too was asking her to *please* call him. Sincere decided to call when they got checked in at the hotel. She knew Keisha would want to take shower after being on the plane for so long.

They arrived at the hotel and got checked in. Keisha had her clothes off and was heading toward the shower before Sincere could tell her what was going on with Michelle and all of the messages. She followed Keisha toward the shower when Keisha stopped dead in her tracks and said, "What's wrong?" Sincere told her she wasn't really sure, she just knew she had deleted a ton of messages from Chance and the last call was from Michelle's doctor, who was apparently asking her to call him as soon as she could. Keisha suddenly felt very insecure in their unofficial relationship, but she didn't hesitate in telling Sincere to call the doctor while she headed in for her shower. Sincere felt a strange, nervous feeling come over her as she listened to the message again to get his phone number. Her stomach sank to her feet as she dialed the number.

"Psych Ward this is Dr. Philpot how may I help you, he answered?" *Did he really just say "Psych Ward?"*

She quietly introduced herself and told him she was returning his call about Michelle Atkins.

"Aw yes, Atkins, Michelle, one moment please while I head in my office to discuss this patient with you."

Okay, Sincere said. This can't be good.

"Yes, Ms. James, I did phone you about Mrs. Atkins; her husband thought you may be able to assist us in nursing her back to life."

Sincere interrupted him.

"Don't you mean nursing her back to health and not life?"

"I understood what I said when I stated it to you! Mrs. Adkins has her health at this moment, her life is what needs saving. She is alert most days, yet she refuses to eat or drink. Her husband brought her through the emergency room last week in a not-so-good state. He complained of long crying and staring spells, excessive weight loss and disinterest in her children. The first two are normal if in an unhappy relationship, but the disinterest in her children is the most troubling. Having suffered from postpartum depression after Christa and CJ, we are all very concerned."

Sincere interrupted Dr. Philpot.

"I have yet to understand how any of this concerns me at this point. She made a decision to return to that unhappy environment! We all have to live with the choices we make and have to learn to live with them!"

Dr. Philpot said, "I couldn't agree with you more; however, her husband thinks you can help!"

Sincere didn't understand how he thought she would be able to help her but Sincere was open to listening.

Keisha exited the bathroom and entered the living room to make sure Sincere was ok. Sincere placed the call on mute as well as speaker so Keisha would know Sincere was completely in the dark. Dr. Philpot suggested Sincere possibly coming to the hospital to visit her, and Sincere adamantly refused. Keisha, took her hand and asked her how she would feel if something happened to Michelle and she was in the position to help her and didn't? Sincere replied, "Well since you put it like that, I would never forgive myself!"

Sincere agreed to visit after the trip under one condition. Dr. Philpot said, "Okay fire away!" Sincere agreed to come to see her, but only if her husband is not around. Sincere wanted to bring Keisha with her for support and Keisha screamed, "No way in hell am going to visit a damn psych ward to see the bitch that broke your heart!"

Dr. Philpot thanked Sincere for her time in calling him and said, "I will see you in a few days, then!"

Sincere hung up the phone, now turning to look at Keisha. Sincere said, "Ok, now with that out of the way, what can I eat?" Keisha was no longer in a playful mood. The phone call proved to more than she could bear after all.

Day 2 in Vegas...

They had not yet managed to have sex during this trip as Keisha became more and more distant. Sincere took Keisha by the hand and let her know she understood the uneasiness. She explained that she too was afraid but was adamant she couldn't go back to someone that hurt her as badly as Michelle had. She looked up at Sincere as she fought back her tears and said, "Sincere, look I know I was for sure the rebound chick that managed to last longer than expected, and I can accept that. But what I can't accept is you pretending you have no feelings for Michelle or her well-being!"

Sincere was crushed knowing she had now lost Keisha because of Michelle and this latest stunt. After dinner, Keisha cut the trip short as neither one of them were able to really enjoy themselves. They checked out of the hotel and boarded different planes, going away for what Sincere hoped wasn't forever.

Michelle's feeling better now

Michelle sat in the chair at the hospital, now back on the regular floor. Dr. Philpot met Sincere in the hallway. He briefly discussed her progress. Sincere peered through the window and Michelle seemed to be almost back to normal, unless the doctor was tricking her also. She entered her room and almost instantly her facial expressions changed and color began to fill her face. Michelle spoke to Sincere saying over and over again, "You really came to see me!"

Sincere's heart ached to see Michelle that small, because she was already small. But *damn*, Sincere thought her breasts weighed more than anything else on her body. Looking at Michelle now, it was clear her head was the heaviest thing. Due to her excessive weight loss she almost favored Starr Jones, as everything appeared to be sunken or sagging in all the wrong areas. Sincere visited with her for several hours and watched her eat a whole meal. *Wow*, Sincere thought, if all she had to do was visit Michelle to make her eat they should have called her a few weeks ago.

169

The orderly came in to change the trash and took Michelle's tray at the same time. Dr. Philpot entered the room, also happy she had eaten something today; Michelle seemed happier. Chance was outside the room wanting to come in to thank Sincere for coming. Sincere agreed he was able to come in unless he acted up, then she was going to leave immediately. Chance looked at Sincere and said,

"You won."

Confused, Sincere said,

"Won what? Michelle is not a prize to be won."

"She chose you over her family," said Chance. "How can we ever move past that?"

Michelle, now feeling strong enough to talk, let him know how she felt about the rules and conditions on her being there, and she admitted that was what caused her mental breakdown.

Dr. Philpot looked at Chance.

"Maybe I was wrong about you being a good guy. You can't make someone stay with you through threats of violence, blackmail or imprisonment. People will be with you if you treat them with respect and humanity."

He pushed his way past Chance before he could respond to him. Sincere stood to leave the room as the nurse was coming in to check her vital signs. Nurse Patton smiled at both of them.

"Your vital signs are much better Michelle, if you keep eating like you did, you may be able to go home by the end of the week."

Michelle smiled at Sincere.

"I'd like that!" she said.

Her smile had a true hidden agenda. Michelle said her goodbyes to all of them and began preparing to leave the hospital by the end of the week. Michelle ordered another complete meal before the end of the night, and she also made sure she was up and moving around on her own each time the nurse came in to check on her. She was watching television and appeared much more alert. Dr. Philpot, pleased with Michelle's complete turnaround, gave her some fatherly advice as she was being discharged a whole day sooner than expected. He spoke calmly to Michelle, "No matter what, always live for what makes you happy, and be there for your children, no matter what!"

She thanked him and said she planned to do just that. Chance was there to pick her up. This time he had no demands, he asked her, "Where to?" She looked in his direction as if looking right through him and said, "Take me to wherever my children are!" He eagerly complied.

Discharged and feeling better, Michelle enjoyed spending the day with her children, especially when Chance wasn't around. Once in the house the welcome home was anything but ordinary. The children waved at her when she entered the house but no one ran over to greet her like she was expecting. Michelle's feelings were hurt but she fought hard to not let it show. She walked into the living room where they all seemed have been sitting. She sat on the sofa next to CJ, but not wanting his mother next him, turned and said, "So Michelle, how long until you leave us again? Or will you be here for Christmas?"

Michelle's heart was breaking at the sound of his voice, but before she could respond Tyler hit CJ so hard for disrespecting his mother in front of him it took him a minute or two to catch his breath. The boys passed licks back and forth until Chance came in the room to check on Michelle.

He was really trying to be a better husband and friend to his seemingly fragile wife, but deep down he felt it was no use. Michelle needed to get away from them to see Sincere for just a moment to see if she still loved her. *Damn*, she said, remembering Cadence had her SUV thanks to Chance.

Michelle found comfort playing with Christa. Christa set up a tea set on the deck with real tea and animal crackers. They both dressed in costumes with a pair of Michelle's old high-heeled shoes.

Chance peeked out and sighed in relief. It seems like she is coming back to us, he thought to himself. CJ wasn't as accepting of her constant presence and told Chance he knew she was going to leave them again, so why bother getting attached to her! Chance didn't bother to correct his son because he felt the same way.

Tyler, on the other hand, was his mother's son and loved her whether she was there or not; he just wanted her happy, even if it meant his parents weren't together. They shared a bond many people only dreamed of or imagined.

Cadence came in the door, grabbing Chance by the collar to get him outside before Michelle saw her.

"How in the fuck did that happen?" Chance demanded from Cadence looking at the huge dent to the driver's side door and front bumper. She said repeatedly it was there when she came out of Macy's. Chance rubbed his head not sure what to say or do. He knew Michelle was going to have a fit that Cadence wrecked a vehicle she wasn't even allowed to drive.

Tyler went out on the back deck to sit with his mom and sister; he just wanted to be near her in case she really was only there for a short time again.

Michelle came in the house to use the restroom when she heard them plotting on how they were going to tell Michelle her SUV was wrecked. Michelle went into the restroom as they were coming in the house. Neither of them said a word about the wreck!

Back to normal

Michelle walked into the kitchen where she could tell they were whispering about something they didn't care to share with her. Before they could even attempt to lie to her, she walked over to Cadence and demanded the keys to her SUV. Cadence looked at Chance for approval; she didn't even look his way when she let Cadence know if those keys weren't in her hand by the time she counted to three the dent in her bumper was the last thing they both would need to be worried about. Not willing to test her on the threat, Cadence handed Michelle her keys.

Michelle turned to face Chance, placing her hands on the center island. She asserted her authority, telling him as long as she was in this house and everything was solely in her name, shit was going to run according to her rules.

Tyler, hearing his mother squaring up against his father and aunt, was hysterically laughing on the inside.

Chance appeared to be a bit startled by the authority in her voice, but he didn't bother to object to her new list of rules that she placed in effect that very instant.

Michelle walked in the bedroom now occupied by Cadence and gave her one hour to get the hell out her house. CJ walked past her mumbled under his breath, "Look who decided to show up playing mommy again!" Before CJ had gotten completely past her, she backhanded him so hard he spun and hit the floor.

Michelle stood over him letting him know who the parent was and reminded him he was the clearly the child. Tyler and Christa stayed outside away from her wrath.

She was back in full force, making her presence known throughout the entire house. Michelle headed to her bedroom to shower and get dressed for the day.

Finally all cleaned up and ready to face the world, she headed towards the door to have some time to herself. She needed to plan her next move to get Sincere back to the Bay Area for good.

Chance sat in silence, clearly bothered she was leaving alone. CJ didn't dare make any comments either, for fear of being struck again. They both watched her walk out the door. Finally free to roam alone, Michelle was pissed about the huge dent in her SUV, but it could have been much worse. Michelle pulled out her cell to call

Sincere. As she dialed the number she paused. What if she didn't want to talk to her, or what if she is with someone else? All those thoughts were going through her mind. *Fuck it*, she thought, then dialed the last digit. The phone began to ring. *Please answer*, Michelle mumbled.

"Hello," Keisha answered. Michelle went from happy to seeing red instantly and demanded to speak to Sincere. Keisha laughed it off saying,

"Well she's in the shower right now. Are you still in the hospital or can she call you when she gets out?"

Michelle snarled back at her,

"I'm out but you need to give her the phone right now, it's important!" Keisha took the phone to Sincere and muted the line, letting her know it was Michelle calling. Sincere unmuted the phone.

"Hello, how are you?"

"So you were fucking her the whole time weren't you! The same time you were lying to me and fucking me. I can't believe I trusted you Sincere, you ain't no better than Chance!"

The cursing and screaming continued for several more minutes before Michelle turned it around and

177

apologized for flipping out. Sincere looked the phone like, *this bitch really is nuts.* Sincere then went on to explain to her she wasn't sleeping with her the whole time she was with her. She did admit to fucking Keisha before they left but it only happened once. Hell, why give accurate numbers? Once sounded better than twice.

Michelle was quiet on the phone. Sincere could tell Michelle was still pissed, but what could she do, she was married and had no plans of changing that anytime soon. Michelle changed the subject, saying, "Well, it's almost New Year's and I'd like to spend it with you. Can you please come here just for the holiday, and I won't bother you anymore? I just need to see you, Sincere!"

Sincere held the phone, unsure of what to say or how to respond. Keisha had been Sincere's rock throughout this whole ordeal; she couldn't hurt Keisha the way Michelle had repeatedly hurt her, but Sincere also knew she needed closure with Michelle so she could officially move on with her life. After a long silence Sincere agreed to come for New Year's only and she was leaving the very next day.

Keisha entered the room emotionless. She just stared at Sincere like a deer in headlights. Sincere took

Keisha in her arms letting her know they both needed closure. Keisha stood completely numb and unresponsive.

Usually Sincere would fix it with sex, but she wasn't in the mood. Her mind was all over the place while on the inside she felt empty. Sincere didn't want to hurt anyone, nor did she want to end up alone.

Keisha changed all of their plans that day and decided she needed some time to think about what was going to be best for her. Sincere prepared to cook dinner, and she overheard Keisha purchasing a plane ticket back to the Bay Area. Not again, she thought, here goes another one out of her life just like that. Keisha ended her call after going over her flight itinerary one last time. She walked in the kitchen and said, "Sincere, it's time for me to go. I can't continue to sit on the sideline wondering when you are going to go back to her; we both deserve better!"

Opening her mouth to speak, Keisha placed her finger over Sincere's mouth to silence her so she could finish what she was saying.

"I'm not upset, I know you love us both at the same time, yet the love is different. You have a real connection to her and I'm okay with that. Your first true love is

179

always the one you remember no matter how badly they treat you. I'd rather we part with no bitterness between us so we can remain friends!"

Sincere agreed and accepted her wishes. She watched in silence as Keisha packed up her belongings.

While driving Keisha to JFK Airport, they talked endlessly like old friends. They laughed about the good times before Michelle even entered their lives. Pulling off the exit, they abruptly ended the chatter as Adele's *Someone like You* flowed out of the radio. Tears welled in their eyes simultaneously.

She slowed down to reflect on their last days that led up to this now sad one. She took Keisha's hand and began to cry as she sang to her. She grabbed her purse and pulled up to the ATA's check in line as the last chorus rang, "Never mind, I'll find someone like you, I wish nothing but the best for you two, don't forget me I beg. I'll remember you said, sometimes it lasts in love and sometimes it hurts instead!"

This was truly a hurtful way to say goodbye to Keisha. Sincere now had this song stuck in her head as she walked in the airport. Keisha, not wanting Sincere to see her board the plane to leave her as Michelle had recently done as well several months prior, left Sincere in the walkway of the gate.

She managed to pull herself together long enough to get back to her apartment. Sincere's cell began to ring, and going by the ringtone, it was Michelle. Sincere answered it quickly, wanting to yell at her for ruining her life yet again. Before she could start in on Michelle, she burst out crying. "What's wrong, what's wrong?" Sincere repeated over and over again. Between her breaths it sounded like she said Chance had raped her, and she wasn't going back to the house, and she was coming to her right now. Sincere told her to pull over at a store or something instead of driving. Michelle agreed and pulled over at the next exit. Angrily, Sincere said, "Michelle I'm on my way," and hung up the phone. Sincere thought she must be really as fucked up in the head as Michelle, or deep down she liked the drama also.

A serious dose of instability rang in Sincere's ears whenever she was associated with Michelle. "Yes, I must be crazy", she whispered to herself. "How and why am I willing to go back to the same bitch that left me, all the way on the other side of the country?" Here she was about to pick up and leave everything for this bitch yet again. She'd been told lust, often confused with love, made you do some crazy shit, but damn, how much was she really going to put herself through before enough was enough!

Just as she was getting ready to pour herself a quick drink, her cell began to ring. Running over to grab it, Sincere screamed, "How the hell did this nigga get my number again?" Sincere answered it as rudely as she could when she saw it was Chance.

"Hello," she angrily answered!

"Hey, Ms. Lady how you doing?" Chance responded. Was this nigga serious? They weren't friends or cool like that for no idle form of chit chat.

"What's up?" Sincere asked him to let him she was in no mood for his mess right now.

"Well I can't find Michelle, so I was wondering if you had heard from her?" he chuckled.

"No, I ain't seen her nor do I have her on my SPS, sorry!" SPS was what Sincere called Sincere's Position System.

"SPS like GPS," he repeated "cute, real cute," he said. "All right, well if she pops up in your presence, let her know the children are looking for her to watch a movie with them like she promised."

"Yeah, okay," she responded. Really? The children are looking for her to watch a movie? He really was a pitiful ass excuse of a man to put this shit on the kids. "I will let her know if she shows up on my radar," she said, as she slammed the phone down. Man, she really needed to rethink this mess!

She wasn't really willing to head back to that shit after being cleared from it. She decided to go ahead and fixed herself a drink to relax before she headed to the office to get some work done. Work was always the best stress reliever next to sex for her. Finishing up her drink she got dressed and headed out the door to her truck. Waiting for the elevator door to open, she checked her cell to respond to a message from Keisha.

Hey babe, just wanted you to know I made it to the Bay in one piece. Don't work too hard tonight! ☺

Damn, they all swore they knew her so well, she laughed. The door opened on the elevator, and she was still looking down at her phone typing when she almost bumped into Derek.

"Heads up" he said. "I'd hate to see you fall in the water fountain or something."

They both laughed it off.

"Must be a good conversation," he said.

"Yes, it is!" Sincere responded.

"Where you headed to this time of night all dressed up? I know you aren't going to work this time of night," he asked, clearly being very nosey yet wanting a real response.

"Well if you must, Mr. Nosey Neighbor, yes I am heading to the office to get a few things finished!"

"Hmm,", he said, "all that work and no play would leave my dick super lonely," he grinned while stroking his crotch.

"Well, that's the difference between men and women, now isn't it," she angrily responded. Luckily women don't focus on sex like that. When it came to sex, Sincere had it coming to her from all directions without any work on her part. Laughing and walking away, he said,

"Well, I may have ninety-nine problems, but getting pussy ain't never been one!"

"Be that as it may Derek, this conversation has been fun, but I need to get going." Derek slid in,

"Well don't forget you still owe me that neighborly nightcap!" Sincere forcibly opened the now closing elevator.

"Let me be really clear Derek, I am not the least bit interested in a little nightcap with a man that revealed he fucked my girlfriend while I was at work, not to mention he watched us have sex on various occasions. Seems a bit inappropriate to me don't you think, Derek?"

She released the hold button to allow the door close before he even had an opportunity to respond.

Derek, laughed and said, "Ok, shit, this one here got me, but she wants me too, oh this fa sho I know. I will hit that before the month out, one way or another," he vowed to himself.

It's about to get real

Sincere was certain Derek was in his apartment thinking of a way to get her to have that nightcap with him.

"Not a chance in hell," she said out loud as she drove through the security gate. Driving down I-95, she got another text from Keisha:

Hey babe are you working or asleep?

Sincere called her back instead of texting. Sincere let her know she was glad she made it back in one piece and she was missing her already. They chatted about the flight, she also told Keisha about the run-in with the neighbor Derek bugging her about the nightcap.

"Be careful," rang out of Keisha's mouth with a bit of concern at the end of it.

"I'll be cool, he's not crazy!" Sincere said in a nonchalant tone. Reluctantly, Keisha said,

"Ok, just please be careful."

They talked for a little while longer, then Sincere got off the line as she pulled into the office parking lot.

"Dammit," she said when she saw lights on as she pulled up on the property. Who in the hell is here this time of night, besides my dumb ass, she thought as she entered the code to unlock the main doors.

Walking to her office she saw the copy room lights were on with a few set of feet walking back and forth before stopping in what she believed to be the copy machine. Not her business, so she headed to her office and closed the door behind her quietly to keep from disturbing them or vice versa.

Sincere thought she could hear music. What was going on in there? She wanted to go see but, she knew she better not get involved in it. Whoever it is appeared to be walking towards her direction. Aww shit, here we go!

Her office door opened slowly; it was Lisa!

"Good evening boss lady," she said, obviously intoxicated or under the influence of something. "What are you doing here this late?" Lisa asked her in a matter-of-fact tone. Sincere was in a mild trance from her clearly after-office-hour attire, a crouchless lace teddy and red heels, too stunned to speak on anything.

Sincere was speechless.

"Hello, Sincere, anybody home? Why are you here?" Lisa asked again in a mildly annoyed voice.

Sincere snapped out of the trance to answer her question with a few questions of her very own. Sincere responded,

"I have work to get done before tomorrow, but furthermore, why are you here after office hours and dressed like that, and lastly, who else is here with you?"

Before Lisa could lie, Sincere caught a glimpse of a man's silhouette and quickly brushed past Lisa to see who else needed to be let go today. Lisa, sensing she was about to be fired, grabbed Sincere's cellphone off the desk and immediately started taking pictures of herself in Sincere's office and on various pieces of furniture in compromising positions.

Sincere lost whoever it was, so she headed back to her office just as Lisa was texting the pictures to herself.

Sincere yelled,

"What the hell are you doing with my phone?"

Lisa, now with a newfound arrogance, pulled Sincere close to her and said,

"Just a little insurance boss. If you don't tell I won't tell I was ever in your office, you got me?" and kissed Sincere on her pissed off lips before leaving her office.

What am I going to do? This bitch got her good, she had to admit that. But Sincere loved a challenge, even ones that started out kind of rough. So this bitch wanted to play, Sincere was down, but she always played to win.

Sincere sat back in her chair and put a plan together to get just what she wanted from this bitch. She'd had many women approach her over the past several years since dealing with Michelle, some of whom she ended up fucking. Most decide if they're throwing pussy at you and you turn it down, they will try again, but if you still turn it down, they just might leave yo' ass alone.

Lisa wanted Sincere badly for some reason. Sincere decided to wait until she knew for sure she was leaving before the big payback. Lisa would soon be a distant memory, she thought to herself. Sincere picked up the phone to call Keisha but Michelle was somehow on her line saying she had just touched down at the JFK airport.

"What the fuck?" Damn, that's why Chance called looking for her ass, he knew she was coming back to Sincere. Sincere less than eagerly agreed to come get

Michelle, or she was free to meet up with Sincere at the apartment. Sincere mumbled,

"I'm sure Derek wouldn't mind coming to grab you from the airport."

Michelle acted as if she didn't have a clue what Sincere was talking about. Sincere flaked it off and told her she would be there shortly.

Michelle's luggage was the last to come off the turnstile, which worked to Sincere's advantage. She greeted her with the not-so-usual hug and kiss, more like a hug to a family member you wished you weren't even related to.

"What's the attitude about?" Michelle asked. Rather than make a scene in the airport Sincere said, "We will discuss it once we get in the truck!" Michelle hated when Sincere did that shit, so she decided to make a big scene by screaming at the top of her lungs for Sincere to tell her what the hell was wrong with her before she went another step in the airport.

Sincere stood there humiliated and shocked at Michelle's behavior. Enraged, Sincere grabbed her by her arm and lead her to the truck without further incident.

190

Once in the truck, Michelle was turned on by Sincere's act of aggressiveness towards her. The ride home was in complete silence, a true first for them. Pulling into the apartment, Derek was pulling out at the same time. His faced turned white as Casper when he saw Michelle in the truck. He pretended to be fumbling for something to keep from looking at Sincere directly. Michelle appeared unfazed by him.

Sincere watched for a reaction from her, yet it never changed.

"Why are you staring at me like that?" Michelle asked in an irritated tone.

"Did you fuck him or something?" Sincere replied.

"No, hell naw! Why would you ask me something like that?" screamed Michelle.

"Well, it was my understanding you fucked him the day you left to go back to Chance and you let him watch us fuck on a regular basis!" Sincere hissed back at Michelle.

"Who in the fuck made that shit up?" Michelle snarled back at her. Sincere replied,

"Derek told me all about the day you left."

"Turn this muthafuckin' truck around, we gonna settle this shit right now with that lying-ass nigga!"

Sincere had never seen Michelle so mad in all the years of knowing her. Sincere turned the truck around and followed the tail lights to his cab. Finally stuck at the stoplight, once behind him Michelle jumped out and kicked the glass out of the back passenger door. Derek was completely caught off guard and began to scream, "What the fuck, what the fuck?" over and over again.

Michelle, now heading towards the driver's side, began punching and yelling at him, "You lying sack of shit, I never fucked you and you never touched me!" Derek, stunned by Michelle's reaction, tried to drive off but it was no use; Michelle was enraged and dead set on making him pay for lying on her. Derek yelled, "Lady I'm sorry, I don't know you, I made a mistake!"

Sincere emerged from her SUV to get Michelle off him. By this time several bystanders were watching and NYPD was responding to the disturbance. Michelle, not moved by the attention she was getting, continued to smack and punch Derek. She fought him as if her life depended on it. Sincere thought that for a second or two Michelle must have envisioned Chance's face, judging by the way she attacked Derek.

The first officer on the scene was a large-framed, average-looking black male. He jumped out of his patrol car and single-handedly grabbed Michelle like a rag doll and told her to calm the hell down before he put her ass in cuffs! Michelle complied instantly. The second officer pulled up as Sincere held onto Michelle. This officer was even larger than the first one and he was fine as hell. He had handcuffs at his disposal.

Sincere briefly imagined her and him having a go-around right there in the midst of everything going on when Michelle slapped her across the face to get her attention.

"What? What? What's the matter? What the hell did you slap me for?" she demanded.

Michelle had tears streaming down her face and shook terribly as she spoke to Sincere.

"How could you think I would have fucked him? I thought we were more than that, but I see you don't even trust me!" Michelle spat back.

"Trust," Sincere yelled, "I'm the not one running back and forth between dick when it feels right and spreading eagle for a bitch at the drop of a hat!"

Realizing both her tone and words were extremely harsh she quickly apologized for being insensitive to her situation. Sincere calmly asked, "What did you expect me to think? You left earlier than you were supposed to, you never called me when you were at the airport, nor did I hear from you after you landed. As usual I have to get a call or a visit from Chance when something was wrong with you or you've pulled another disappearing act!"

Michelle shook her head in agreement.

"Ok, I guess I deserve that!"

"No you don't, well, you don't from someone that's supposed to love you as much as I do!" Sincere said as she hugged her tightly.

The first officer was walking over to get Michelle's side of the altercation.

"Hello ma'am, glad to see you have calmed down, so what's your side to this?"

Michelle filled the officer in on what was going on.

"He lied about sleeping with me to my girlfriend right here and caused a serious trust issue between us when all he did was take me to the airport that day!"

The second officer was now laughing with Derek off to the side, and Michelle began to get angry all over again.

The first officer sensed it as well, then cleared his throat and the laughing ceased as quickly as it began. He turned his attention to both Michelle and Sincere and said,

"Well, given the statement from the gentleman over there, it was a grave misunderstanding and he doesn't want to press charges at all, so you're both free to go."

Sincere quickly grabbed Michelle's hand and placed her back in the truck. Silence played again on the ride back to the apartment.

Pulling in the garage, Sincere wondered how in the hell Derek seemed to have beat them back when they had clearly left before him. Sincere didn't question it. She left it alone for the moment, even though it was really bothering her. Sincere needed to keep Michelle as calm as possible. They entered the apartment still in silence;

195

Michelle looked around the apartment trying to either pick up an unfamiliar scent or find something out of place. Unable to find anything wrong, she retreated to the bathroom and ran some bath water.

"Would you like to join me?" she asked Sincere.

"Why yes, of course I would," Sincere replied.

They both headed towards the tub when it dawned on Sincere she hadn't kissed Michelle at all since she picked her up. Sincere pulled Michelle in her arms and began to kiss her softly on the lips, making her way to Michelle's neck, shoulders, and settling on her breasts.

Michelle tried to push her away but decided not to fight Sincere.

"I missed you so much," she whispered as Sincere slowly walked her back to the bed, putting the bath on the back-burner. Michelle forced herself to relax, trying not to think about who else may have been in the bed. She only knew of Keisha and thought maybe Lisa, but she had no proof. Forcing the images of Keisha and Sincere out of her mind, she was finally able to fully submit to Sincere.

Kissing her breasts and rubbing Michelle's body, Sincere gently moved her hands down the side of her left thigh. She settled her hands on the pie shaped nectar. She rubbed and parted Michelle's moistening lips with only one finger. Michelle's legs parted with ease once the invitation of more to come had been extended.

Without any hesitation, Sincere settled her head in the perfect resting place, directly in between Michelle's legs. Her tongue quickly met Michelle's eagerly awaiting lips and they soon became one! Licking and sucking her wetness, Sincere felt her nipples harden while her inner walls throbbed with mad intensity.

Tonight's session was met with a true purpose from many different angles. Sex with anger involved was almost better than make-up sex. Sincere prepared for Michelle to straddle her when she was rudely interrupted by a hard knock on the front door. Attempting to ignore it, she picked up her pace when there was an even louder knock. This sound was a bit familiar; it sounded almost like a bang or thud of a baton.

She placed Michelle back on the bed and went to the door. Peeking through the peephole, Sincere was startled to find it was both officers from the scene of Micelle's beating of Derek. Sincere grabbed her robe and opened the door. "Good evening ma'am, may we come in?"

First Lisa, now Derek

The first officer entered the apartment, looking around slowly. He looked Sincere up and down and asked where her girlfriend was.

"She's in the bedroom where I left her until we were so rudely interrupted!"

"Which one?" asked the second officer, while proceeding down the hall toward the closed bedroom door.

Sincere rushed in front of him to stop him.

"Ummm, excuse me what the hell are you doing? You can't just walk in my house, this is not *Rip the Runway* and I know you need a warrant!"

Hearing all the commotion, Michelle emerged from the bedroom to see what was going on. The second officer smiled and said,

"Everything is fine ma'am, I was just making sure you were okay. We received a call about screams coming from this apartment. Are you ok?" Michelle chuckled at the indication she was hurt.

"I'm fine, but I would have been better, had you not interrupted us," flashing her killer smile in Sincere's direction.

The first officer laughed at her response.

"Okay well try to keep it down and you two have a good evening!"

The second officer stood there dazed.

"Is there anything else we can help you with, Officer?" said Michelle.

As the officers were leaving, Sincere saw Derek in the hall smoking and looking in her direction. She smiled.

"Hope you're enjoying the view, you nosey muthafucka!" she said. Michelle slammed the door saying he wasn't worth the time or the energy. Sincere stood there for a moment, remembering the beating Michelle had given him at the stoplight and he appeared to be completely normal, not a scratch on him. Michelle, noticing her daze, touched Sincere's arm.

"Is everything okay?"

Sincere could no longer hide it,

"No, something isn't right about this!" She swung her door back open to get another look at Derek but he was gone. The stale smoke smell was also gone as if they both vanished in thin air. She came back in the apartment to find Michelle going through her cell phone with a look of confusion filling her face.

Michelle threw the phone at Sincere's head. She caught her phone before it hit the wall and Michelle was now right in her face. Snatching the phone out of her hand to prove her point, she screamed:

"So you fucked her at work, huh Sincere!"

She had no idea what Michelle was so upset about. *Oh shit, the pictures.* She had completely forgotten about them. Lisa's ass would surely be made to pay for this shit here. How could she have been so stupid to have not deleted them?

"Michelle, please listen, it's really not what you think, and I never touched her!" Sincere continued trying to plead to a not-so-understanding Michelle. She explained she was at work when she initially had gotten her call to pick her up from the airport. Sincere stated,

"She had only been there for a hot second, honest." She admitted she saw Lisa at the office, apparently she was fucking around with a man there in the copy room, and she was going to try and blackmail her because she knew she was going to get fired. "Please believe me, Michelle," she pleaded, holding out her cell phone. "Please just look at the text message sent to my boss earlier!"

Michelle was pissed beyond comprehension, but she read the message she was asked to read.

Hey Kirk, I came in the office to clear my head and caught Lisa here with an unknown person, but I didn't get a good look at him. I ran after the person, and upon my return Lisa was snapping pictures of herself with my cell phone in a desperate attempt to frame me. Please respond once you get this message, I'm heading to the JFK to grab Michelle, and she just landed!

Man, was she glad she always thought to cover her ass. Michelle handed her back the phone and looked back at her like, *okay, bitch you got off this time*! Wiping the invisible beads of sweat off her forehead, she sighed in relief. The mood was for sure killed at this point. Her body temperature was about as cold as the water in the bathtub.

Michelle stood in the balcony light with the moon glistening off her frame. Sincere became easily aroused all over again wanting to taste the sweetness of her nectar.

She lowered herself on all fours to crawl over to be at the level she most admired when dealing with Michelle sexually. Michelle pretended to not be interested, so Sincere moved away from her. She would never be labeled as the one who made one do what they didn't want to!

She loved Michelle for many reasons: she was smart, sensual, and sexy as hell. She had the ability to make a mop and bucket appealing to a slave under her every command. The one thing Chance and Sincere each agreed on was Michelle's ability to make them do whatever she wanted, even when they knew it was wrong or they just didn't want to do it!

Michelle pulled Sincere back to the right level then whispered, "Take me Sin, take me now!" Her body in full agreement as her own inner juices began to flow, she softly pulled on Michelle's lips and purred right on cue. Sincere loosened her robe with the one free hand for the light to glow off her inviting breasts.

If Derek was watching them now, Sincere was surely not going to disappoint her audience. She pulled every trick out of the bag and Michelle was a willing participant to each touch. Her cries grew louder and louder as Sincere entered her from behind with two fingers in each opening yet still managing to suck on her inner lips.

Michelle began to buck like an untamed bull not wanting to be saddled or caged. Out came the loudest cry along with gushiness from her wet walls and back door. Michelle smiled in amazement. *Where did that come from babe* look written all over her face. They'd never been that in tune with one another. Michelle excitedly kissed Sincere while sobbing at the same time. Sincere's invisible wings took form again. Yep, that nigga never made her do anything close to that!

Derek was also right on cue, watching from the top of the roof, jacking himself off to completion when Darnell, his twin brother walked up.

"So was it as good today as any other day?" he laughed, patting Derek on the back. He angrily snatched his boxer shorts over his eight inch penis and walked away. Darnell caught up with him, finally able to see the full extent of the damage Michelle did to his face. Derek said,

"Damn bro, she really fucked your face up didn't she!" Darnell had to agree.

"Yeah, she got off but it's cool, it's not the first time a bitch hit me because of your ass. So when are you going to tell Michelle about your little problem?"

Derek laughed at the notion of doing the right thing by anyone but himself.

"Man, screw that dyke bitch, I ain't telling her shit!"

Darnell couldn't believe what he was hearing. He looked at him with pure disgust, which was reflected in his tone.

"You need to tell her you are HIV positive before she possibly passes it off to her girlfriend or anyone else!"

Derek grabbed Darnell by his neck and told him:

"If you say anything to her or anybody else I will fucking kill you!" Darnell swore not to betray his brother as they both went back into their apartment through the open fire escape.

Michelle woke up from a sexually induced drunken stupor; tiptoeing in the bathroom, she relieved herself and moaned as if having a mild orgasm. She peaked out to make sure Sincere was still asleep. She paced back and forth contemplating her next move. *How am I going to get her away from here before he sees her alone?*

Not realizing Sincere was now standing in front of her, she began to talk to herself out loud.

"If I tripped on her possibly fucking that bitch Lisa, how is she going to react to me really having slept with Derek!"

Sincere interrupted the conversation with herself before Michelle revealed anything else she may not have wanted to be known.

"Just tell me the truth is all I ask!" Michelle cried but felt a weight being lifted off her shoulders once she had finally told Sincere everything. She had in fact sleep with Derek. She also admitted she knew it was the twin she attacked, but she was afraid to let Sincere know for fear of her being upset.

Sincere just sat there unmoved; she knew in her gut all this time she wasn't crazy when their eyes met briefly when he was in the hall smoking. Michelle tried to rationalize it, and Sincere abruptly cut her off with one question, "Did you use protection, Michelle?" Those five words were the only words that mattered to her right now. Michelle's response was anything but what she wanted to hear. "I don't remember," rolled off her tongue as fast as she had lied about being with him in the beginning.

"What the hell do you mean you don't remember?" She screamed grabbing Michelle by her neck. "You could have potentially killed all of us by being careless, Michelle," Sincere said, letting her go. Michelle ran in horror; Sincere had never been so angry toward her.

Sincere hurriedly got dressed to go grab an at home HIV kit from the corner pharmacy. Michelle sat there repeating over and over again, "What have I done?" Sincere wanted to spit on her, but she couldn't bring herself to do it. She grabbed her keys and left for the store.

Michelle decided she could at least get cleaned up then straighten up the room so it would be clean when Sincere came back. As if a cleaned up house and pussy was going to change the fact she slept with this nigga unprotected. The bitch in her wanted to beat her ass, but Sincere let the woman in her handle the volatile situation.

Sincere called the one person she knew she could depend on, Keisha. She answered on the first ring in an unusual tone.

"Hey Sin," Keisha said. Hm, she rarely called her that. "What are you doing?"

Sincere asked her as if she had the right to be mad if she had company. Sensing an attitude, Keisha said, "Calm down babe, I'm actually on the other line with your friend Michelle! She just called me and I thought it was you, So is there anything you want to tell me before I click back over?" she said in a not-to-be-played-with tone.

Completely caught off guard, Sincere shrugged her shoulders.

"Naw, we good. Michelle is there; she got there after I was working earlier. She just popped up unannounced!"

Michelle hung up and called Keisha right back.

"Ok babe," said Keisha, "it's whatever right now, let me take this call from her and I will call you back in a sec!"

Keisha hung up before Sincere had a chance to respond. What is going on? Everything seemed to be falling apart right in front of her. She pulled up at Rite Aid to get the kit before her embarrassment kicked in.

The moment of TRUTH

Sincere wasn't just mad at Michelle for sleeping with Derek, she was more mad at the irresponsibility behind it. Sincere bought the kit and bumped *Shit* by Future all the way back home to drown out her thoughts.

Michelle had no problem submitting to the test; unbeknownst to Sincere, she had already been tested when she returned home. Michelle went through with the test right along with Sincere and said, "Expect the worst but hope for the best, right?"

Was the bitch for real? She wasn't ordering fast food from a new restaurant, this was real life Russian Roulette with a lethal dose of HIV loaded in the chamber. Sincere took her test and walked away, staring at Michelle with a sense of disgust. Her head was pounding now. She turned to the best solace when frustrated: music. She turned on some quiet music, and out poured Troop *Still in Love*! "Yeah right, not today!" She turned it off as quickly as it came on. She closed the bedroom door, now playing Mike Jones *Scandalous Hoes*. This seemed more appropriate for the current situation. Granted, she herself was going back and forth between Keisha and Michelle.

Sincere knew her status and Keisha's as well. Keisha called back as Sincere showered. Michelle came in with the cell phone and, hearing the song on repeat, she purposely threw Sincere's phone in the toilet and flushed it.

Damn near falling out the shower, Sincere stuck her hand in the toilet to get the phone. Fire in her eyes, she pushed Michelle out of her way to throw her phone in some rice.

"What is your damn problem?" Sincere growled at Michelle. "You are the one that slept with a complete stranger who may have only God knows what and you have the nerve to have a damn attitude because someone called me. Let me correct that, the same person you called when I left was merely returning my call for me to tell her to get tested just as a precaution." Reminding her that's what responsible people do, and that children hide their shit then throw tantrums when they get caught.

Michelle had all she could take of Sincere's mouth. She jammed a stack of papers in Sincere's face dated for the morning after she went back to Chance with a bunch of different tests on them. Sincere walked over to the bed to read it.

The lab work had Michelle's name written on the top with every STD known to man listed. The paper listed showing she had been tested and confirmed a negative status on every STD screening performed. Skimming through the paper showed HIV labs also confirmed on page two, yet she only gave Sincere page one. "Where is page two, Michelle?" Sincere screamed at her. Michelle walked over to her purse to retrieve page two, sobbing, and handed it to her. HIV results: non-reactive. Sincere shouted, "Thank God!" at the top of her lungs. Sincere knew hers would be also since over the last several years she had already been getting tested every 6 months as a precaution. Sincere kissed her and apologized for treating her that way.

That night Sincere decided to base her decision on returning to the Bay Area squarely on her test results. The results are in; tests reveal they both were non-reactive. Blowing out a sigh of relief, they packed up the apartment that evening. The following morning they both headed to the office to turn in the keys to both the apartment and Sincere's office.

Heading out of the apartment one last time, they bumped into both Darnell and Derek. Michelle stopped dead in her tracks when she came face to face with Derek. They stared at one another as if in an Old Western gun battle. Sincere held Michelle's hand tighter and said, "It's okay babe, we faced it together and we will move on past it as one." Derek agreed as he laughed, "Sounds like a plan, she will need the all the care she can get when it hits her!"

"When what hits her?" Sincere asked him, dropping Michelle's hand. Derek said:

"Well now seems to be a good a time as any to let you know, I'm HIV positive. I'm making it my mission to fuck as many of you lesbian bitches as possible to rid the world of you dykes!"

Darnell stood there in silence as if battling with an inner demon of his own. He had just about enough of his brother's bullshit and couldn't take it anymore.

"Um excuse me ladies," with as much masculinity as he could muster up! They all stopped arguing and took notice of his tone and very timid frame.

Darnell looked his brother and said:

"I can't do this anymore, this lie is killing me! I switched the tests results, I am the one that is HIV positive, not you. I just wanted to get back at you for always teasing me for being gay. Ladies, I am very sorry for all of the problems we may have caused either of you, please forgive me!" He quickly ran off to their neighboring apartment.

Derek stood just as dumbfounded and speechless as they were. Instead of apologizing, he strutted off, zipping up his True Religion jeans. They both dodged a bullet that day and silently vowed to never do that shit again.

They were eagerly heading to the office to turn in the keys to the apartment and then head off to the office; hopefully they wouldn't have any more surprises on the way out of there. The office was just about to close for a tour when they walked in to turn in the keys to the now-vacant apartment. Stacey, the apartment manager, pretended she was sad to see them go. Sincere already knew better; this was more for business and less personal. She never gave a white woman the time of day and wasn't about to start right now. She left a forwarding address where she could forward any future correspondence along with her security deposit. Stacey expressed understanding and walked out right behind them.

Since they were leaving the area the following morning after turning the keys, they checked into a hotel room near her soon-to-be former office. Back on I-95, they went to the office for the last bit of the unfinished business. The mood was anything but happy when Sincere walked in to turn in her office keys. Everyone in the office wore the same look of gloom on their faces. Sincere asked what was wrong and they looked as if she had a plague of some sort. She went to Kirk, the director, and asked him what the hell was going on. An employee was found dead this morning in the copy room with a note apologizing for a laundry list of things she had done. Sincere immediately looked around the office for Lisa. She searched every inch of the office, including the basement storage, and Lisa was nowhere to be found. Assuming Lisa was the person found, Sincere felt almost relieved to have her out of her life and unable to bother anyone else anymore. *Dammit*, she knew it was too good to be true when Lisa walked up behind her. "So I hear you were searching for me, is that right boss lady?"

"Well," Sincere said in a shaky tone, "I actually was just making sure it wasn't you."

"If you think I'm going to let you get away with playing me like that, you got another thing coming," said

Lisa." Kirk waltzed over just as she hissed her words at Sincere.

"Aww Lisa, just the person I was looking for!"

"Good morning Mr. Carter," she cheerfully replied.

"Lisa, would you please step into my office, I'd like to have a word with you. Ms. James, if you will please come as well as this involves you also."

"Yes, Mr. Carter, after you sir," Sincere replied. Not sure what he was going to say to either of them, Sincere just knew she was clear from any wrongdoing.

Mr. Carter asked both of them to take a seat as he closed the door.

"Ladies, I have asked you both to come to my office to discuss an incident that apparently took place yesterday evening."

Sincere began to feel uneasy in her seat, just as did Lisa. Mr. Carter went on and on about sales, then he sternly looked at Lisa and spoke about office politics and fraternization on the job. Oh wow, was she about to be accused of fucking this broad when she did nothing of the sort, even though she was all but throwing that it in

Sincere's direction every time she saw her? Lisa chimed in: "Sir, I can explain!"

Kirk cut her off.

"No need Lisa, as they say, 'big brother is always watching!'

Aww, shit what the hell was Kirk talking about? Who was watching them? But before anyone had the opportunity to elaborate or question Kirk any further, there was a knock on the door. Tamara, Kirk's receptionist, entered the room and let Sincere know Michelle was waiting in her in the office. Sincere thanked her and smiled in Lisa's direction. Kirk said:

"Thank you Tamara, let her know we won't be much longer!"

"Okay sir," she mumbled and quickly closed the door behind her.

"Again ladies, I called you both in her regarding a problem. As I already stated, 'big brother is always watching.' For security precautions, we have off-site cameras running in this office at all times, which also happens to pick up voices as well."

He stood up from his chair, grabbing a television remote of some sort.

The picture that almost completely covered his wall disappeared at the push of a button and countless screens came up showing angles throughout the entire office. Sincere's eyes fixated on the screen showing Lisa standing naked in her office. Feeling exonerated, Sincere said,

"Yes, he got her!"

Sincere grinned from ear to ear on both the inside and the outside. Lisa looked as if she had just seen a ghost. Sincere moved her eyes to a few screens over and saw Lisa in the copy room with a man that looked a lot like Derek, but she wasn't quite sure.

"I knew it," she said out loud.

Kirk turned and said:

"Calm down Ms. James, you will have a chance to speak in just a moment!"

Sincere relaxed in her seat, even surer she wasn't going to have any sexual harassment crap thrown her way.

Lisa leaped out her seat and said:

"Look if I'm being fired just tell me so I can get my stuff from my desk!"

Kirk looked at Sincere and said:

"The Human Resources person should be here shortly. I know you all have a few things to take care of. It should be just another moment Ms. James."

Sincere briefly excused herself to let Michelle know it would be just another moment or two. Michelle wasn't bothered at all; she was eating the doughnuts and drinking coffee the company had provided to help the staff deal with the loss of the female coworker. Sincere still had yet to find out who it was.

Lisa gets exposed

While leaving her office she literally bumped right into the HR person and decided to walk in with her as somewhat a united front. Sincere allowed the HR rep to enter the office first and proceeded in behind her. Lisa looked as if she had seen a ghost when she laid her red watery eyes on Becky Harris.

Becky extended her hand to Lisa and Sincere then took a seat at one end of the table. She opened her notepad and begin to jot down who all was in the room along with a few other things. She pulled her eyeglasses down to the tip of her nose and spoke about why she was there and what the role Human Resources was for in a meeting such as this.

Lisa interrupted her, asking was she getting fired. Becky spoke over the rude interruption, stating:

"I am here to listen to the facts and make the best recommendation for all involved."

Becky asked Kirk to bring her up to speed as to where they were in everything thus far. Kirk cleared his throat and asked Becky to direct her attention to the screens on the wall that were stuck in freeze mode.

Sincere sat there snickering on the inside, waiting for the element of surprise. Becky walked over the screen displaying Lisa in the copy room with a male figure, possibly Derek. Also, a few screens over showing her in Sincere's office in her teddy the same day apparently.

Wait a damn minute, were her eyes deceiving her? Sincere saw a glimpse of Kirk's office at the top with Lisa straddled across his lap, clearly naked and riding him long and hard. Kirk noticed Sincere's eyes fixed on that screen and tried to divert the attention away from the screen and back to Lisa in general.

Sincere almost felt bad for her, like she had been set up almost. Sincere was asked to speak about her few interactions with Lisa, even the situation where Lisa was naked in Sincere's vehicle. Luckily she refused to get in or this could have gone a totally different route.

"Ms. James, or is it okay call you Sincere?" said Becky. Sincere nodded,

"Yes it's okay for us to all go by first names, we are all family, right?" Sincere asked with a sneaky grin.

Becky grinned as well.

"Ok, well with all the formalities out the way, let's get on with it, shall we?"

Becky went on to say, given the information she had received from both Kirk and Sincere, she'd first like to extend the opportunity for Lisa to speak if chose to.

Lisa was no longer paying attention; she already knew she was about to be fired so she said:

"Do whatever you need to, just let me get me own belongings from my desk is all I ask!"

"Okay, since you are choosing not to say anything on your behalf, I will move on to Kirk. He was more than eager to spill the beans in a desperate attempt to save his job. He went into detail about his unfortunate run in with Lisa, leading to him succumbing to her sexually and the bribery involved."

Hell, Sincere was glad she declined all her advances like a maxed out credit card. This shit got bad really quickly for both of them. Becky adjusted her eyeglasses on her face properly, then there was another knock on the door. Several security guards sporting black suits and wireless ear pieces entered Kirk's office and everyone fell silent.

"Ms. James, can you please come with us?"

"Me!" she screamed. "What the hell did I do? I may be the only person in this office that didn't fuck this bitch!" She shouted before forcing herself to calm down. Not wanting to draw attention to herself, she asked, "Am I being fired?"

Becky hesitated in her response.

"We think it's best for you to return to your office at this time while I advise Mr. Carter and Lisa of the company's decision concerning their employment."

Sincere rose from her seat and headed back to her office where Michelle was now sleeping on the small corner chaise. Sincere woke her up and filled her in as quickly as she could about the events inside Kirk's office.

Michelle was pleased to find out Sincere really hadn't slept with Lisa. Sincere was also glad she didn't so much as touch her ass, no matter how hard she tried.

Becky terminated both Lisa and Kirk as soon as Sincere left the room. One by one they were shamed by walking the long haul out of the door with security guards escorting them straight to their cars and following them off the property. Once they were out of the parking lot and no longer visible, Becky knocked on Sincere's door.

"Thank you Sincere for being a noble employee and upholding standards set for our company."

"There is no need to thank me," said Sincere. "I have one reason alone to abide, and it's more than your company standards."

Michelle thought Sincere was speaking about her until Sincere said:

"My life means more to me than a quick roll in the bed with anyone, regardless of how nicely the package is presented."

With regret, Sincere informed Becky she was actually just here to turn in her keys because was returning to the Bay Area today.

"Oh, Sincere I'm sorry to see you go. Given the events you have had to endure while here, I will make note in your file you are able to rejoin our firm should you make it back this way or we expand to your area." Becky was visibly saddened by Sincere's decision to leave.

Sincere thanked her for the kind words. She found herself unable to leave without knowing a little bit more about the employee found dead this morning in the copy room. Becky paused.

"Oh I'm sorry, I thought you were aware, it was Crystal from the mailroom. She hadn't been with us very long but she and Lisa were very close."

Prying now, Sincere asked if she knew what happened or what may have led her to want to end her life in the office of all places.

Becky, not wanting to get involved with the office politics and gossip, figured what the hell, Sincere was leaving anyway. Apparently, Lisa and Crystal decided to have a sexual rendezvous here last night with a cab driver Lisa was seeing and that things got out of hand. However, the word in the office is the cab driver flipped out and told Crystal he was HIV positive and she decided to end her life right here after having unprotected sex with him and Lisa.

Michelle and Sincere grabbed each other's hands as they both said "Darnell" at the same time.

"I'm sorry, Darnell? Is he employed here also?" She pulled out her notepad again. "No, he doesn't work here; he is the cab driver, or it may have been his twin brother Derek. We had a few words with both of them before we came in this morning. Strictly off the record, Becky, someone needs to suggest to Kirk he get tested for HIV just as a precaution."

Becky looked mortified at the thought of even discussing the possibilities with Kirk. Becky wondered if her own husband had come in contact with Lisa like Kirk did. She quickly excused herself and wished Sincere the best of luck in her endeavors as they made their way back to the Bay Area.

The walk to the truck was truly bittersweet. Sincere had officially closed each chapter here and they were on their way back the Bay Area. She called her family to let them know she was on her way back to the Bay and she was coming back to stay until a new opportunity presented itself.

Heading back to the Bay

The typically long ride back seemed to be making a new record as they breezed through each city like it was nothing. Michelle was anything but silent; she made plans on getting another apartment as soon they touched back down in the Bay Area. Sincere didn't offer any suggestions after everything they had made it through in New York. Sincere didn't want to pour salt or sand in anything.

She was learning to live in the moment. Tired of driving she pulled over to a hotel so they could get a little rest and maybe get a little nookie in also...just maybe. Sincere left Michelle in the truck while she checked in to the Marriott hotel off the Ohio state line. Looking back, she realized she had become a traveler since dealing with Michelle.

Sincere began to chuckle as she left the hotel lobby. Her phone vibrating in her pocket interrupted her thoughts. She glanced at the caller ID before answering it just in case it was Chance or someone else she didn't care to hear from.

The smile that formed on her face meant only one thing: Keisha!

"What's up with you, babe?"

Keisha sounded a bit down and with good reason. The condo she had been staying in was being condemned by the State for code violations, and she only had 30 days to get out of there.

Sincere told her she was on her way back to the Bay Area with Michelle and offered to let her stay with them one way or another. Keisha said

"Are you smoking crack, Sin, Michelle is not ever going to allow us to be under the same roof!"

Sincere grinned.

"Leave Michelle to me Keisha, I'll call you tomorrow! Let me get her out of this truck before she sends out a search party looking for me in the damn lobby."

They both laughed as Sincere ended the call while heading out of the door. Michelle was freaking I Spy Private Eye; she asked who she was on the phone talking to before Sincere sat down in the truck. Sincere saw no reason to lie, so she didn't! She told her it was Keisha saying she was in need of a place to stay because the State was condemning her spot in the next month. Michelle mumbled, "Hm, how fucking convenient!"

"What's that babe? Did you say something?" Sincere asked with authority in her voice.

"No, nothing at all," she said at first with a hint of attitude in her voice. Sincere took Michelle's hand and said:

"Look, she took me and my children in until I left with you, and I have to return the same favor!" Sincere promised Michelle, "It won't be for more than a few weeks a month at the longest." Michelle, now feeling overly confident when she spoke this time, said:

"Oh, I'm not worried about it being a long-term arrangement!"

Sincere ignored her; she was tired and just wanted to rest after a shower.

They both showered and ordered room service. Sincere went to the bar for a few shots of Patron to help her relax and sleep a little heavier. Michelle waited for her to return; she had a cake baked for her.

Sincere staggered back in the room a few hours later in hopes of catching some sleep. Michelle pretended to be asleep. Sincere moved about quietly to keep from waking her. Sincere undressed and slid in the bed.

Michelle lay completely naked under the covers as she slid her body directly up against Sincere. She propped her leg over Sincere's body as she began to play with her breasts while fingering herself. Sincere slowly rose up. Who does that when you have someone next to you willing to do whatever you desire? Michelle was super horny and she thought Sincere wasn't in the mood because she kept saying how tired she was. Sincere found Michelle's willingness to please herself very enticing. She watched as Michelle slowly slid her fingers in and out of her own lips then placed the same fingers in her mouth so she could taste herself. What a definite turn on.

Sincere lay there watching Michelle now caressing her own breasts. Sincere leaned down to kiss her lips and Michelle moved, pushing Sincere flat on her back and said, "It's my turn to really do you, Sin," Michelle said seductively. Sincere continuing to lie there, waiting to see what Michelle decided to do next. She closed her eyes, and then slowly opened them when she felt Michelle slide out the bed.

"Where are you going babe?" Sincere asked. Michelle replied:

"Just wait and don't move."

She returned with a few lit candles and placed them on the nightstand then climbed back in the bed.

What was she about to do with those candles? Michelle kissed from Sincere's toes right up to her pie. She turned around facing the wall and straddled Sincere's waist. Sincere could see nothing but Michelle's bare ass as she leaned forward making it just possible to do a 69. Sincere got ready to take her in when she suddenly feel something extremely hot dipping just above her navel.

This was that shit she liked right here. "Do all the wild shit you like! The wilder the better," she moaned. Michelle threw her head towards Sincere and asked,

"Is this what you like?"

Before Sincere could open her mouth to answer, her nipples were covered in candle wax, and the tingling sent so many sensations through her body. A faint scream crept from

Sincere's mouth as she reached to grab a hold of Michelle's ass and began to lick her right down the middle.

The more wax Michelle poured, the deeper Sincere went. Before long her enter face was buried deep. Michelle began to stiffen her back as she sat straight up, allowing Sincere to breathe more than just her juices. They changed positions to kiss one another passionately as they drifted off to sleep without eating the food they ordered from room service.

Michelle tried again at the food bit and ordered them both some breakfast. Nothing too heavy, but just enough to keep them from falling asleep on the road. They still had quite a bit of distance to tackle. Michelle packed up their belongings while Sincere checked out of the room.

Once again the damn phone began to ring as Sincere was at the front desk, only this time it wasn't Keisha; it was her son, Jay.

"Hi, Mommy," he yelled in the phone.

"What's going on lil man? Mommy misses you guys so much."

"I miss you too mommy, guess what?" he said.

"What?" she answered.

"Chyna's dad enrolled us in school yesterday and today is the first day!" Wow, Kevin actually did something without needing her help, she was shocked.

"Hey lil man, put Kevin on the phone!"

"Ok, mommy, here he is," he said.

Sincere could see the smile plastered across his face. Kevin got on the line,

"Hey ma, what's good with you?"

"Oh, not too much of nothing, Kevin. I'm heading back to the Bay. I was just letting you know and also wanted to see if you had a problem keeping the kids for me so they won't have to be moved again once I get settled."

"No problem," he answered, "I wouldn't have it any other way! Now what about Jay, that's Lamont's son, he may want to keep him but then again that nigga ain't even calling this lil dude back. So either way it's up to you, but he's cool to stay. But you will have to finish enrolling him as soon as you touch back down here."

Sincere thanked him again said her goodbyes to Kevin and her children. *What the hell?* Michelle was actually in the driver's seat, this was a true first.

"Was I taking too long checking out?" She asked, jumping in the passenger's seat.

"No, not at all, I'm not driving with Miss Daisy through the mountains, you will be asleep," she said. "No I won't, we just woke up!"

Michelle grinned and said:

"Oh yes babe, you will be asleep shortly, drink your coffee!"

"Hm, did you put something in my coffee? Should I be scared?" Sincere asked in a nervous tone.

"Sin!" she yelled, "Drink the damn coffee and relax. You always drive and I know you can't stay awake if you are over here so it works, so just go with me, okay!"

Feeling helpless, Sincere did as she was told and drank the coffee. Within 30 minutes flat she was knocked out, which was before they hit the first tollbooth. Sincere had all sorts of dreams during this ride back to the Bay. In the first dream, they were all living in one big house in Fayesville, right outside the Bay Area, which is where Michelle was looking at anyway.

They being Michelle, Keisha and Sincere, plus all of their children under one roof. This dream was cut short when Sincere was rudely awakened by Michelle swerving to avoid something in the street.

"What's going on?" Sincere said with panic in her voice.

"Nothing babe, go back to sleep before you get car sick. The mountains are right up the way."

Oh crap, Sincere just knew she was past them by now but oh well, guess not. She reached in the backseat for her iPad and headphones to tune out any noise and also to keep her ears from popping since she forgot to get some chewing gum.

She reclined her seat and tried to get back to the same dream she had before. No such luck, the next dream was more of a nightmare. She kept seeing visions of Chance with his head blown off and the children screaming. Sincere woke herself up this time and decided to just wing the ride through the mountains. She looked around trying to figure out where they were. To her surprise they were already out of Ohio and entering Indiana.

Michelle and her lead foot weren't playing. They each had a purpose in trying to get back to the Bay. Sincere missed her children terribly and Keisha needed her help. Sincere needed to work on when she was going to really discuss this arrangement in detail with Michelle.

Michelle must have ESP or something. She turned the music off and said:

"So let's talk about what you said last night."

"What's that?" Sincere asked.

"We talked about a bunch of stuff last night Sincere!" she yelled while shooting her the *don't fuck with me* face. Sincere opted to not continue to play dumb.

"Keisha," she blurted out. "Yes, let's talk about Keisha and her suddenly needing a place to stay right as we are so conveniently on our way back to the same area."

"Look Michelle, she said--I know this all looks bad, but keep in mind I had no idea you were coming to New York either yesterday. You just popped up, not that it was a problem, I'm just putting it out there though!"

"Okay, you got me," Michelle admitted.

"So bottom line, what are we going to do?" Michelle knew she helped her out when they were going to leave, but Michelle felt like this was different, kind of suspect, even. Michelle pleaded her concerns.

Sincere agreed the timing was a bit off and questionable, but the fact still remained that she was going to help her in any way she could.

Viva, Las Vegas

They drove through several more states almost as fast as lightning. The radar detectors were working overtime. Making an overnight stop in Las Vegas, Sincere thought, what the hell, you only live once. They checked in right on the Las Vegas Strip at the Luxor. The room was okay; nothing to write home about, but it was workable. After all, who plans on being in the room except to sleep and fuck anyway? The concierge checked their bags and said, "They will be in your room when you return and welcome to Las Vegas!"

Man, one could get used to treatment like that! Sincere thought while pulling Michelle closer to her as they headed out amongst the thousands of people in the desert heat. Today was a record 85 degrees, perfect for this time of year. Right after New Year's seemed like an all right time to go as any, since it wasn't too hot out.

They enjoyed walking up and down the Strip, taking in the sights and even discussed attending a few shows later that night. They walked both the old and new

Strip for hours before stopping for a bite to eat. Michelle wanted to try Bubba Gump Shrimp, so they did. Sincere was all for eating, but she preferred something more familiar to them. Michelle started complaining about Sincere not trying new stuff since they weren't at home. Sincere agreed and ordered something along the lines of lobster baked mac n' cheese. It sounded different and she loves mac n' cheese when it's made the right way. The server also mentioned it was still considered Happy Hour so all drinks were $2, including specialty drinks. Both their eyes lit up as Michelle ordered the first set of drinks.

Good thing they were walking everywhere because this was about to be a no-drive-anywhere situation for sure. After round three or four they decided to leave and head back to the hotel room. Drinking and walking proved to be more difficult than either of them had expected. They clung to each other like Siamese twins maneuvering as one body. They made it to the hotel after the long walk back. Once in the room they both collapsed in the bed, missing the Criss Angel show that was scheduled for later that evening.

The hotel room alarm clock started blaring several hours later. "Shit, morning already?" Sincere said while nudging Michelle. Both were maneuvering through the room with serious hangovers, a small drawback from drinking cheap drinks with no limitations. Michelle staggered around just as badly as Sincere.

They needed to get back to the Bay, but neither of them was in a condition to drive at the moment. After they showered they drank the worst black coffee ever presented to a human being not currently in prison. The hotel coffee was pure motor oil of the highest quality octane. Sincere officially banned Michelle from going near a coffee pot.

Checked out and ready to tackle the last 5 hours, Sincere stopped off at the nearest Starbucks for a true cup of coffee to offset what Michelle had tried to make earlier. *Starbucks in hand, sunglasses on with Bonnie riding shot gun.* They smiled as they headed down the road, then that bitch ass nigga Chance called Michelle's cell. She answered with an attitude like no other. Sincere, only picking up one side of the conversation, thought he must have been trying to hold the kids over her head again. Her voice developed some serious bass when she yelled, "I don't give a fuck what you tell them anymore! I hate being there with you and I will take you to court over my visitation, so again I don't give a fuck!" *Damn*, Sincere said to herself.

Michelle hung up with him shortly after and he didn't her call back this time. All was quiet inside the truck and outside on the road. Riding the last few hours they made idle chitchat, avoiding the obvious conversation about Chance.

Finally unable to talk about anything else pointless or meaningless, Sincere asked Michelle if everything was everything. Immediately regretting the fact she even bothered to ask her, Michelle started in hard, going from the beginning, around the moon, and through the mill before finally getting to the gist of the conversation between her and Chance. Sincere pretended to be interested although she really couldn't care less. She merely just wanted Michelle to be okay.

Sincere headed straight to see her children when they got to the Bay Area. Michelle sat there in the truck in a trance for a good minute, then she finally got out. She grabbed the baby, Chyna, and gave her the biggest hug and kiss. Chyna was surprised to see Michelle as she squeezed her tightly around her neck. Chyna nearly choked on her candy she was chewing in her mouth when Michelle grabbed her. Jay stood staring off into space, not even realizing Sincere was there. "Jay, come here lil man," he blinked as he headed directly for Sincere, grabbing her waist tightly. Kevin, hearing the commotion, stepped out on the front porch to see what all the noise was. He spoke to all of them before pulling Sincere directly away from the kids.

"Sincere," Kevin began, "The kids want to stay here with me for good."

Sincere looked back at her children as they played with the neighborhood children now convening in the street. Tears formed in her eyes. She knew it was best, at least until they found a new place for them to stay.

Sincere stayed there a good hour or so before her cell rang. It was Keisha checking on how the journey was going. She let her know she was visiting with her children and she would call her back once they left. As Sincere ended the call with Keisha, she felt Michelle burning a hole in her back with her eyes.

"What's wrong babe?" Sincere asked.

"Who was that on the phone?" Michelle asked.

"It was just Keisha checking to see how the road trip was going." Sincere responded.

"Oh, is that all she wanted?" Michelle hissed back angrily. Sincere kissed her children and they drove off.

Michelle stared out the window in complete silence. Sincere refused to say anything to her to keep from having an argument about a past lover who needed to stay with them. Michelle hit the dashboard with her fist.

"So this bitch still needs to stay with us I guess, huh?"

"Yes babe," Sincere answered, "It won't be more than a few weeks, I promise. I will be helping her find a new place in the meantime, just give me that, please!"

Michelle shook her head in agreement.

It's moving time

Michelle glared at Sincere out the corner of her eye for a good while before screaming:

"This one is perfect!"

Startled, Sincere asked:

"What's perfect? Why are you screaming?"
Michelle sucked her bottom lip and said:

"Pull over right now!"

Sincere pulled over as she shoved her phone in Sincere's face. She slowly took her phone and looked the ad for a home lease option in the area they were looking at. The house was perfect for her children when they visited as well as Sincere's when they came back home.

The house also had a finished basement, which in Sincere's mind would be used for Keisha to stay there temporarily. Sincere gave her the okay to call for them to see the house today if at all possible. She told Michelle not to get her hopes up, because the house cost a lot more than what she was willing to spend monthly, even though it was perfect.

As they pulled into the driveway, they were met by a small framed Asian couple. The man shook their hands and proceeded into the front door behind them. Michelle and Sincere each removed their shoes and put on booties. He looked at his wife and smiled as if relieved they removed their shoes. Sincere shot Michelle a look like,

Yes, Asian nigga, we do have manners!

Once past the foyer area he gave them the okay to look around the house. He and his wife waited for them by the door. Michelle was already halfway up the stairs when Sincere caught up to her. The second level was beautifully lit, and each room was extremely spacious with ceiling fans already installed. The master bedroom was the best for Sincere. Even though the money was an issue with her, she loved the house. The master bedroom took up one entire side of the house, equipped with matching walk-in closets separate from the dressing area, with a built- in chaise lounge seat.

The master bath was immaculate. Sincere especially admired the glass doors from the floor to the ceiling with multiple jets on each wall. Visions danced in her head of the fun she could have with Michelle and Keisha, if given the opportunity. The bathroom also contained a large claw tub, as if from the vintage days, standing on four raised legs from the floor. Making their way down the back stairs they ended up in the kitchen. Sincere smiled from ear to ear.

"This house is awesome," they both said out loud.

"You like?" asked the Asian man as they walked around the kitchen. Sincere turned back seriously and said,

"Everything seems in order, give us a little more time to finish looking around the house and I'll be with you in a few moments!"

More spiral stairs led to the finished basement equipped with a full wet bar and theater seating along with three separate rooms that could also be used as additional bedrooms. "Damn, babe, it even has a freaking bathroom with a tub and shower. My children would have their own space when they come over to visit."

Seeing a glow on her, Sincere took Michelle in her arms and began kissing her passionately as if no one else was there in the house with them. Michelle tried to push her away, but failed miserably. Her body wanted everything Sincere wanted to give her at that moment.

Sincere placed her on the wet bar gently tugging on her jeans with her teeth. No real time to devour some much needed lunch, so she with a more subtle approach settling for a quick tug and pull. Not wanting to move away or get caught as she heard tiny footsteps heading towards the stairs, she gave one more piercing bite covering Michelle's mouth to muffle the scream. Michelle leaped off the wet bar and tried to straighten up her clothes before they saw them and failed miserably.

"I presume you like?" the Asian woman asked with a crooked grin on her face.

"Oh yes, I like and I like and the house is nice too," Sincere said laughing. The couple looked confusedly at one another. Michelle grabbed Sincere's arm and said,

"Let's go discuss it before someone takes it from us!" Everyone headed back to the main level when a few more people were parking right in front of *their* house. Sincere looked at Michelle and asked:

"Do you want it, like it or love it? And do you think everyone will be happy and comfortable here?"

"Yes to all of the above!" Michelle yelled while pushing Sincere toward the Asian man who was now showing other people around the house.

"Oh, hello again, you want house now?" he asked. Trying not to laugh at his accent, Sincere said:

"Yes, we both like the house and would like to take possession of the house now or as soon as it's available!"

The Asian man waved at his wife to get something and mumbled in another language as she took off toward their car. Sincere looked back at him as if to say, *what the hell did you say for her to beeline like that?* The Asian man asked Sincere:

"How much you got to put down today?"

"I have enough!"

She loved to wheel and deal and this house was going to be her best deal ever. They all sat at the table, sliding offers back and forth until Michelle and his wife drank and entire pot of tea. The two finally agreed to a rate that was feasible for both sides so neither felt like they got played or fucked with no Vaseline.

Moving day, they both got up early from the hotel and headed to the house to start setting up shop. Keisha called Sincere's cell, no answer. She then called Michelle on hers looking for Sincere. Michelle threw Sincere the phone to talk to Keisha, very apparent she was madder than shit. Sincere let it go; today was going to be a good day, no matter what! Michelle stood within earshot of Sincere talking to Keisha. Sincere, sensing Michelle was there wanting to know what they were talking about, put Keisha on speaker to put Michelle at ease.

Sincere had already given Keisha a few code words to let her know when Michelle was listening to their conversation. Keisha picked up rather quickly and kept the conversation focused on her needing to find a place to stay. She reiterated she would only be in the house for a very short time. Sincere let her know she was on speaker so she could maneuver around better. She then asked if she had found a new place yet or did she still need to stay with them for little while.

Keisha had found a place, but she still needed to stay with them for about for two weeks; Michelle nodded okay. In Michelle's mind, shit, two weeks was always better than no date at all. They exchanged all the details and ended the call. Sincere thought Michelle was mad, but she seemed relieved, almost happy even. Sincere continued to watch her for a little bit before getting in the truck and heading to the house to meet the movers.

Everything was moved in a couple hours of as Michelle and Sincere set up things one room at a time. She felt like Michelle just wanted to keep an eye on her, but she quickly shoved it out of her mind as being paranoid. They decided to leave the kids rooms for last and decided to call it a night to make a quick dinner.

While Michelle made dinner, Sincere made herself a drink, one shot of Patron to settle her nerves. She knew Keisha would be arriving any minute and she had to brace herself for the unexpected. *Ding, dong,* went the doorbell. Michelle nearly jumped out of her skin slicing the vegetables. Sincere said, "I'll get it babe, calm down, it's just Keisha I'm sure!"

Muthafucka, it was Chance with their children to see Michelle.

"Hmm, Sincere, looks like you did pretty good maintaining the lifestyle my wife was used to having when she wanted to be a mother!"

250

The children disregarded his comment and ran to Michelle with open arms. CJ walked past Michelle and sat on the bar stool, texting with his headphones on, not even bothering to speak. Sincere walked over and tapped him on his shoulder.

"So you not speaking to anyone today?" Sincere asked him. CJ stood up, smirking,

"What's good, Sincere? Hey Mom, nice place," and placed his headphones right back, not inviting a back and forth conversation.

Michelle chose not to allow his disrespectful ass to ruin the day. Instead she played games with Christa and Tyler for a moment. Chance stood there looking sideways as Sincere finished the dinner Michelle had started. She felt his eyes roaming her entire backside and soon felt a burning sensation. Sincere spun around before he could close his mouth.

"Is everything okay from your view?" Sincere said smiling.

"Yeah, Sincere, everything is good."

Ding, dong, went the doorbell again. Michelle shot Sincere the *go get it* look. She headed toward the door; this time it was Keisha and Chance's current girlfriend Tameka. Keisha walked in the door as if she had been there since day one, plopping down on the loveseat in the family room off the kitchen.

Michelle turned towards Sincere and snarled, "You better go check that bitch, she is only visiting here!" Sincere nodded, grinning on the inside, *here we go*, the longest dreaded and shortest stay in history. Feeling the obvious tension from every angle in the house, Sincere took Keisha on a small tour to allow Michelle a little time with her children. Keisha smiled devilishly; she was more than eager to go in separate area of the house to escape the evil glares from Michelle.

They disappeared to the upstairs area for a small tour, avoiding the master bedroom. Cardinal rule number one: when you have a woman you have been intimate with, never take her in the bedroom that you now share with another woman. Bad for current and future business as well as sexually, unless they all agree to do it together.

Now heading down the back way to the kitchen, they continued to the basement.

"This is where you can stay until your place is ready," Sincere said with a grin.

"Hm, will you be able to tuck me in at night, Sin?" she asked. Feeling a bit uneasy, Sincere ignored her comment and said,

"On that note, this will conclude the rest of the tour!" Sincere turned and started heading toward the stairs when Keisha grabbed her hand.

"Calm down babe I was just kidding, unless you really want to tuck me in at night!"

Sincere pulled away, pointing:

"Michelle is upstairs, are you crazy? She will have both of our asses for dinner with no regard for how she skins us, especially yo ass!"

Now feeling a bit bad for having convinced Michelle everything was cool for her to stay, Sincere was having second thoughts. She had slept with both of these women countless times, yet she had a different type of love for both of them. They both went back up the stairs before Michelle sent out a search party. Michelle was standing by the basement door as they walked up the stairs. Chance and the children were all leaving. Yes, just in the nick of time!

Keisha started putting her belongings in the basement. On the last load of clothes before she started on the furniture, she nearly knocked Sincere into the wall as she staggered through the walkway with an armful of clothes.

"Damn, you could have at least said move or asked for some help!" Sincere yelled. She decided to step out and help her so she could get it over with a little faster and most importantly she wouldn't tear up shit. She looked relieved as Sincere helped her grab the king size mattress off the truck. Their hands grazed one another as Keisha whispered:

"This is a new mattress," with an innocent wink. Oh shit, Sincere could see where this was heading.

Sincere put her mind in fuck mode heading into overdrive. She wondered how she could get both of them upstairs at the same time. She knew she had to convince Michelle it was her idea and get Keisha to go along with it.

In the basement they placed the bed on the rails when they began kissing. Like clockwork Sincere heard

Michelle's footsteps heading in their direction. Sincere headed towards the door leaving Keisha to start organizing her stuff alone.

Dammit, just as she thought, Michelle met Sincere at the door with her hands on her hips.

"So, how's it going?" she asked with a slight attitude. Sincere said:

"Fine, do you want to help? It would go much faster you know."

Michelle tugged at her boy shorts as she bit her bottom lip. Hm, Michelle wanted Sin to fix her right now! She pouted.

"Right now babe I'm helping Keisha move the rest of her stuff off this truck so I can shower and lay it down," Sincere said in a mildly agitated voice.

Pretending to stomp off Michelle went down to the basement to see exactly what Ms. Keisha was doing down there all this time. Michelle entered the basement, amazed to find all the clothes Keisha had organized by color in her closet, shoes included.

"Wow," she said as she walked around Keisha's room. "I see you have some really nice taste in clothing also," Michelle said.

"Yeah, I do okay," Keisha said feeling eyes roam all over on her. "Some say I have an eye for nice things," she whispered.

Michelle sat on the bed admiring how nice and comfortable it was. Suddenly, thoughts of all three of them in one bed rolling around entered her mind.

How can I get this going, she wondered

Keisha was a very attractive woman; hell, Sincere has already tested the waters with Keisha, she thought to herself. Maybe, just maybe she could also!

As Sincere gathered the last bit of stuff from the truck, she noticed it was very quiet in the house and Michelle was nowhere in sight.

"Michelle must be in the shower," she mumbled to herself as she moved toward the basement.

"Last load," Sincere announced while plopping everything down on the floor, clearly exhausted now.

"Hey babe," Sincere said when she saw Michelle on the bed.

Surprisingly they both said *hey* back. Michelle didn't get irritated at all. Sincere saw something was on her mind though as she continued to bite her bottom lip. Sincere asked:

"Babe, you good?" Michelle was deep in thought and continued to stare off into space. "Babe," Sincere said now tapping Michelle's shoulder this time. Michelle was startled, with drool coming out the corner of her mouth. She wiped her lip and said, "Hey babe what's wrong?" Sincere leaned next to her ear and asked, "So what were you thinking about doing?"

Sincere already knew what it was and allowed her invisible wings take form. She already knew Michelle wanted to get with Keisha badly. Shit, who didn't want a sample? Her ass was firm like biscuits and breasts to match, and she surely wasn't hard on the eyes!

Keisha was an all-over dime piece and her lip service was always on point. Yes, Sincere thought to herself, she just might be able to get it from both tonight without even having to ask. Michelle gave her the *you know what I want* look! Pulling Sincere closer she whispered:

"Can I have her tonight?"

Aw damn, this shit was like taking candy from a baby, easy as hell and Sincere didn't have to do anything.

"Keisha, come here babe," Sincere whispered.

"Yes Sin," she answered as she made her way slightly past Michelle.

Sincere spoke softly to Keisha:

"I want you to kiss Michelle for me, babe."

"Here, right now!" Keisha asked.

"Why not? No time like the present, unless of course we should all get cleaned up!" Sincere said, smiling immensely.

"Sure, let's all take a shower together first," she said.

All in silent agreement, they headed to the master bedroom and undressed each other. Michelle started the shower water for all of them. Sincere continued to curiously eye both of the ladies preparing for a good time. They all eased in the shower together with Sincere grinning from ear to ear. Sincere was ready to see who would do what first, if they would like it, and so on and forth. Michelle motioned for Keisha to come closer to her. *Yes, it's about to go down!* Sincere thought to herself.

Sincere was bursting with excitement and anticipation waiting to see what was going to happen next. Michelle leaned over and softly kissed Keisha on her neck with her eyes glued on Sincere the entire time. Sincere nodded in approval as Michelle continued to kiss and fondle Keisha's awaiting breasts. Making her way down to her breasts with her lip, Sincere became increasingly aroused and swimming within her own wetness just from watching the two of them perform.

Keisha's head fell back as Michelle sucked and cupped each of her breasts. She motioned for Sincere to come over to her, her back against the wall as Michelle made her way to her awaiting nectar. Michelle continued to please Keisha. Both ladies were going at it hard. Sincere, feeling left out, felt it was time for her to make her presence known as she entered Michelle from behind.

Michelle gripped Keisha's ass cheeks for balance. Coming up for air as the water turned increasing cold they all climbed out of the shower one by one. Michelle asked for *Dylan*, a ten-inch dildo equipped with a large rabbit attached to it. "Oh, yes," Sincere grinned. They were preparing to give Keisha the true lesbian experience of her life.

She grabbed Dylan and stood within comfortable reach two sets of wet lips. Keisha sat with her eyes closed, unable to believe this was really about to happen. Michelle fondled her breasts as Sincere made her way to Keisha. Her eyes never opened but her mouth surely did. She placed her warm tongue in the middle of Sincere's wetness. She licked until her face was covered with her juices.

Michelle sat back watching as Keisha pleased Sincere in so many ways with her tongue. Now feeling her legs grow weak, Sincere eased her body from Keisha's mouth and motioned for each of them to retreat to the bedroom.

The Bedroom

Keisha left the bathroom first, heading for the bedroom. Michelle and Sincere both hung back for Sincere to whisper a few directions to her.

"Hey babe, let's really show her what goes down in here!"

Curiosity always killed the cat and tonight, right here, Sincere was truly about to bury any preconceived ideas she ever had about a female threesome. Sincere had been with many women; she always thought an all-girl threesome was just too much pussy in one room for her. However, she was slowly changing her tune on that, considering she was loving how everything was playing out so far.

Michelle placed Keisha in the middle of the bed as she and Sincere both took their positions around Keisha. Michelle took it upon herself to place her head between Keisha's legs and softly licked her lips one at a time. Keisha's eyes began to roll, indicating she was enjoying the service she was receiving. Perfect, they both were enjoying one another; time for Sincere to go in for the kill.

Sincere placed Dylan in her mouth to get him wet enough to enter Keisha from behind. She slowly parted Keisha's ass cheeks and licking her sweet, wet nectar briefly along with Michelle as their tongues touched one another. Keisha began to quiver as Sincere placed Dylan in slowly, her body lightly jolting.

Michelle was in her zone and was about to bring it home when Sincere placed two of her fingers in her mouth for some extra lube to penetrate Keisha's forbidden hole. Sincere slowly inserted one finger and her body completely relaxed. Sincere moved her finger back and forth, in and out to get her ready for the second finger to enter gently.

Dylan was still inserted and doing exactly what Sincere needed him to do when Michelle told Keisha to slowly turn on her side. Surprisingly, they all kept the rhythm and Dylan stayed in while everyone repositioned themselves. Sincere really loved Michelle, she had set the stage for the most perfect 69 ever. Keisha lay on her side as Michelle positioned her tiny frame to line up perfectly against hers. Michelle looked Sincere in her eyes and said,

"We gotta do her right, baby!"

"Yes babe, we gotta treat her all the way, right!" Sincere replied. With all three of her holes occupied, Keisha was no longer able to control her muffled cries and had completely pushed Michelle's body to the side as she began to scream as she came from both her ass cheeks and her wet walls. Her body went limp as she drunkenly moved her hand in Sincere's direction to come towards her. Keisha needed to be held by Sincere as she cried in her arms and took in what had just happened to her.

Michelle, now offended, didn't want to share with Keisha anymore! She laid back spreading her legs for Sincere, revealing a bittersweet pearl right in the middle while caressing her own breasts. Sincere looked over at Keisha, "Well hell, she's too tired," so she went to work on her true baby.

She moved Keisha to the opposite side of the bed and went to work on Michelle. Kissing her passionately every place her lips landed, she settled right where her hands directed.

She placed Michelle in the air on top of her as Michelle proceeded to ride Sincere's face. She was careful not to let her cum just yet. Sincere played with her clit and moved away just before she erupted. Keisha slowly sat up to watch Sincere please Michelle. Michelle rubbed, suckled and licked on her own breasts as Sincere moved her fingers in and out of her wet pussy lips and continuously sucked on Michelle's clit.

Michelle let her hair down when she felt Keisha's eyes admiring the scene.

"Hey babe, come over here instead of watching from a distance!"

Keisha crawled over on all fours and settled her body right on Michelle's face. Michelle slowly inserted her tongue into Keisha's awaiting wetness. Keisha must have still been aroused, she began cum almost instantaneously. *Damn* Sincere thought to herself, either Michelle gave head better than she did or Keisha was seriously still worked up from earlier. Keisha climbed down off Michelle and lowered her head as she moved to the top of the bed, shaking her head. Sincere finished Michelle off and headed towards the shower to get cleaned up. Keisha lay in the bed dazed, not moving at all.

"Hey Keisha, come get cleaned up so we can call it a night," Michelle yelled. Keisha didn't budge. Sincere grabbed a towel and lathered it up with soap to clean her up. Wiping herself and Michelle clean she barely had any soap on her when Keisha stepped in the shower as well.

"Damn, babe what's that look about?" she asked.

Keisha cried, she had never experienced anything like that before in her life! Sincere smiled shyly, feeling her wings take form. Hm, I did the damn thing, she thought to herself. Sincere attempted to clean her up and Keisha clamped her legs shut!

"No, I can do it myself!"

"Okay, here you go babe!" Sincere turned back toward Michelle, and it was on again. Michelle stood under the shower allowing the waterfall on top of her breasts. She placed her foot on the handle on the shower door and opened her nectar and began to finger herself while licking her nipples one at a time. Shit, Sincere wanted her all the time. She was more than addictive; she was her poison, she had the ability to make Sincere do shit she didn't want or desire to do. Michelle was that *one* and nothing was off limits to her.

265

As they finished the lovemaking in the shower, Keisha slipped out to use the restroom. She took notice of Sincere on her knees devouring Michelle's juices under the water. *Fuck it, you only live once*, she thought. Keisha dropped her towel in the sink and entered the back of the shower behind Sincere. Keisha moved Michelle's hands off her own breasts and placed them in her own awaiting mouth. Michelle screamed with delight as she was yet again about to cum. Sincere inserted two fingers into her wetness as she took Michelle higher and higher.

The water was cold at this point, so they finished with one another and got cleaned up. All three of them lay in the king sized bed together, touching one another in some form or fashion. Sincere lay in the middle to give her the opportunity to fondle each of them overnight equally. Michelle drifted off to sleep first. Sincere turned towards Keisha and noticed she was sobbing again.

"Hey babe, what's wrong!"

Keisha muttered between her sobs:

"Everything I did here tonight was beyond any of my wildest dreams. I have never felt so good in all my life!"

Surprisingly Sincere didn't get excited about it. She felt bad in a sense for exposing Keisha to the things they had done as a group. They chatted for a few more minutes, then they both drifted off to sleep. Sincere awoke to Michelle tapping her.

"Hey read this, and I'll go see if she's still here!" Michelle skipped out the room as Sincere read the note she had handed her.

"What the fuck?" Sincere screamed jumping out the bed running toward the hallway clutching the note. Sincere ran smack dab into Michelle as they both fell on the floor. She said:

"She's gone babe."

Sincere got up off the floor to finish reading the note:

Sincere,

Last night was great and even better than I could have ever imagined. I think given the recent events I need to stay someplace else. I thank you and Michelle for all your hospitality during my time of need!

I'll be in touch!

Much love,

Keisha

Sincere ran down to the basement; Michelle was hot on her heels. Damn, it was completely cleared out and the keys she had just been given her several hours before were now sitting on the counter. Damn, she really left, Sincere thought to herself. Michelle smiled as she turned her back away from Sincere.

To be continued...

Meet the author

Sincere James is a midwest native of Kansas City, Missouri. As an author of erotic tales, her completed works include Off Limits, which immediately set the stage for the highly anticipated return of drama-filled chaos among several dysfunctional characters in Without Limitations. She initially began writing as a pastime, never expecting for her personal and seemingly private thoughts, let alone her inner secrets, to ever appeal to others to read for entertainment. She has worked in the health care industry for over 15 years. She is a mother of two sons and two daughters who currently reside in Texas. During her down time, she enjoys traveling with her family and relaxing in warm climates. She encourages interactions with her readers in the form of comments and questions and during upcoming releases of her work.

Stay up to date with Sincere James on her website at: www.authorsincerejames.com